PRAISE FOR *THE CITY OF BLOOD*

"At the end, Cassian likens Nico to Georges Simenon's great detective: 'Inspector Maigret can sleep soundly. He has a worthy successor.' Many readers will agree."

—*Publishers Weekly*

"Molay can give CSI writers a run for their money... The book transported me to Paris."

—Marienela

"Classy French police procedural."

—Netgalley review

"A great series set in a beautiful city."

— Reader review

"Suspense lovers will get their fill."

—*Le Journal*

"A taut novel, with likable characters and optimism. Fresh and a real pleasure to read."

—*Blue Moon*

"Magical. Written by a master."

—*Aventure Littéraire*

ALSO IN THE PARIS HOMICIDE SERIES

THE 7TH WOMAN

CROSSING THE LINE

PRAISE FOR THE SERIES

"A highly entertaining and intellectually stimulating read... unreservedly recommended."

—*Thinking about Books*

"If you're looking for a chilling novel that will keep you guessing until the case is solved, this is the book for you."

—*Criminal Element*

"If you enjoy your crime set in a foreign clime, then this is the book for you."

—*Crime Fiction Lover*

"Procedural fans will appreciate the fresh take."

—*Booklist*

"For readers who enjoy a low-key approach with detailed descriptions, Molay is just the ticket."

—*Publishers Weekly*

"Readers will find it impossible to put down. Highly recommended."

—Goodreads

"The kind of suspense that makes you miss your subway stop."

—*RTL*

"An excellent mystery, the kind you read in one sitting."

—*Lire*

"Extremely enjoyable, thought-provoking read."

—*Books are Cool*

"A slick, highly realistic, and impeccably crafted thriller."
—*Foreword Reviews*

"Frédérique Molay is the French Michael Connelly."
—Jean Miot, Agence France Presse (AFP)

"Blends suspense and authentic police procedure with a parallel tale of redemption. Well-drawn characters and ratcheting tension."
—Paris mystery writer Cara Black

"A taut and terror-filled thriller. Frédérique Molay creates a lightning-quick, sinister plot. Inspector Nico Sirsky is every bit as engaging and dogged as Arkady Renko in *Gorky Park*."
—*New York Times* bestselling author Robert Dugoni

Best Crime Fiction Novel of the Year
(*Lire* **Magazine**)

Winner of France's prestigious
Prix du Quai des Orfèvres award

The City of Blood

Blood

A Paris Homicide Mystery

Frédérique Molay

Translated from French by Jeffrey Zuckerman

LE FRENCH BOOK

First published in France as
Déjeuner sous l'herbe
by Librairie Arthème Fayard.
World copyright ©2012 Librairie Arthème Fayard
English translation ©2015 Jeffrey Zuckerman

First published in English in 2015
by Le French Book, Inc., New York

www.lefrenchbook.com

To Anna Kern (poem), Alexander Pushkin,
translated by James Falen, from *Selected Lyric Poetry*,
Northwestern University Press, 2009

Translator: Jeffrey Zuckerman
Translation editor: Amy Richards
Proofreader: Chris Gage
Cover designer: Jeroen ten Berge
Book design: Le French Book

ISBNs
978-1-939474-18-6 (Trade paperback)
978-1-939474-17-9 (E-book)
978-1-939474-19-3 (Hardback)

To the best of all worlds,
Filled with kind people and false criminals;
The world I dream of for my children.

To the students whose paths have crossed mine,
and to their teachers.

Don't take the tableau-piège for a work of art.
It's a piece of information, a provocation.
—Daniel Spoerri

"There is in all things a pattern that is part of our universe. It has symmetry, elegance, and grace—those qualities you find always in that which the true artist captures. You can find it in the turning of the seasons, in the way sand trails along a ridge, in the branch clusters of the creosote bush or the pattern of its leaves. We try to copy these patterns in our lives and our society, seeking the rhythms, the dances, the forms that comfort. Yet, it is possible to see peril in the finding of ultimate perfection. It is clear that the ultimate pattern contains it own fixity. In such perfection, all things move toward death."

—Frank Herbert, *Dune*
from "The Sayings of Muad'Dib"
by the Princess Irulan

1

Footsteps, the stench of a cigar. Chief Nico Sirsky looked up from his files and glanced at his watch: 1:11 p.m. Deputy Police Commissioner Michel Cohen, his boss, walked into the office without knocking.

"If I were you, I'd turn on the news," Cohen advised.

No hello. It was an order. Nico grabbed the remote control and pointed it at the television. The news anchor appeared. Black eyeliner and smoky shadow accentuated her eyes. Not a hair was out of place. In a panel at the bottom of the screen, a reporter was clutching his microphone.

"Just watch," Cohen said.

Directly behind the reporter was the Géode, the gigantic steel globe at the Cité des Sciences et de l'Industrie. The huge Cité complex in northeast Paris encompassed a science, technology, and cultural center, a museum, and much more. It attracted visitors from around the world. Nico raised the volume.

"I can only imagine the consternation there," the newscaster lamented, a touch theatrically.

"Absolutely, Élise. This story has gripped people in France and beyond."

"Arnaud, please bring those viewers who have just tuned in up to speed on this horrible discovery. I must warn those watching that this may not be appropriate for young children."

The camera panned to an open pit next to the Canal de l'Ourcq in the Parc de la Villette.

"Here, at this exact spot, archaeologists, artists, and others started an extraordinary excavation three days ago," the reporter said. "Now that dig has taken a strange and ghastly twist."

The camera zoomed in slowly on the pit. It was possible to make out dirt-covered tables, dishes, and bottles. The shot then turned into a full close-up of an inconceivable sight.

"You see what all the commotion's about?" Cohen asked.

Several men in orange vests were pushing back spectators on the Prairie du Cercle meadow and forming a security perimeter.

The news anchor was talking. "Arnaud, we can hear the sirens. Is that the police?"

"Yes, Élise, officers are arriving now."

Those were the local precinct officers, who would guard the crime scene and take down witness accounts. Normally, they would then call in the public prosecutor and his underlings—"the devil and his minions," as Cohen liked to put it. That was in theory. But this was not a normal situation. The television news had already tipped everyone off, and Nico was betting that Christine Lormes, the public prosecutor, was putting on her coat at that very minute.

"Looks like we're going to be on the news," Cohen said with a note of sarcasm. "We're set to meet the prosecutor in the courtyard. Which squad are you putting on this?"

"Kriven's."

Nico could forget about his sandwich. The week was off to a bad start.

2

Sirsky and Cohen hurried down Stairwell A, its black linoleum worn down to the cement, and made their way to the interior quad of the courthouse complex, where Lormes was waiting for them. From there, they walked quickly to their car, a black sedan with tinted windows. Nico got behind the wheel, while Michel Cohen offered the passenger seat to the prosecutor. The deputy commissioner slipped into the back. Commander David Kriven and his men would follow in other cars. Nico turned the key. The guitar licks of the Young brothers and Bon Scott's raw tenor flooded the car. "Touch Too Much" by AC/DC—a song about a guy going crazy over his girlfriend, or in other words, the story of his love affair with Caroline.

Startled by the music, the prosecutor almost hit her head on the ceiling. Nico switched off the CD player.

"Are you trying to kill me, Chief?" she asked.

"There are worse ways to die," Nico said, grinning.

"Things sure have changed," Cohen muttered. "The head of France's legendary criminal investigation division doesn't wear a dark suit, and he listens to hard rock."

Lormes stared at Nico, taking in his build, his blond hair, and his eyes as blue as the waters of Norway's fjords. He smiled at her innocently. The car made its way out of the 36 Quai des Orfèvres parking lot and headed along the Seine, its blue lights flashing.

"The minister of culture was at the archaeological dig's opening three days ago," she said. "He shoveled the first pile of dirt, just like his predecessor thirty years ago, when they were burying Samuel Cassian's *tableau-piège*."

"Cassian was what they called a new realist in the sixties and seventies, right?" Nico said.

"Yeah, he glued the remains of meals—plates, silverware, glasses, cooking utensils, bottles, and the like—to panels, and art collectors who liked that sort of thing hung them on their walls," Cohen said.

"I remember reading something about his work," Nico said, swerving around several cars. "He was considered an anticonsumerist. He used food and ordinary kitchen items to make a statement about wealth and hunger."

"Cassian was no starving artist, though," the prosecutor said. "He made a surgeon's fortune from his pieces. Then he opened pop-up restaurants and organized interactive banquets."

"In the eighties he got tired of doing the same thing over and over and decided to have a final banquet," Cohen said. "He wanted his guests to bury the remains, and he planned to have the whole thing dug up years later."

The excavation had started a few days earlier, when reporters, scientists, and artists came together to disinter the fragments. They planned to study the remnants and determine the work's sustainability. It was nothing less than the first excavation of modern art.

"This is quite a scandal," the prosecutor said. "Samuel Cassian is a prominent figure. The organizations sponsoring the event are going to go ballistic."

"We'll have to get to the bottom of this quickly," Cohen said.

Nico turned onto the Quai de Jemmapes to go up the Canal Saint-Martin, which was lined with chestnut and plane trees and romantic footbridges. The other drivers slowed down to avoid the speeding sedan. This neighborhood, where the famed Hôtel du Nord still stood and the ghost of actress Arletty lurked, had the feel of prewar

Paris, with bargemen ready to jump the lock gates to the reservoir linking the Villette basin to the Seine.

At the Place de la Bataille-de-Stalingrad, Nico took the Avenue Jean-Jaurès toward the Porte de Pantin. Then he got stuck in a tangle of cars, heavy trucks, motorcycles, and pedestrians wholly unaware of the specific lanes marked for their use. Nico watched the bikes pass him by and leaned on the horn before skillfully weaving through the traffic like a king of the jungle, careful to keep his distance and avoid bumpers and doors. The prosecutor gripped the handhold without emitting the least objection or interrupting their shared train of thought. What *were* human remains doing in the middle of tables, tablecloths, dishes, silverware, the leftovers, and trinkets?

They arrived at the Place de la Fontaine-aux-Lions, across from the Grande Halle, where uniformed men were holding back the crowd and the reporters. Nico parked in front of the Pavillon Janvier, named for the head architect of Villette's former cattle markets and slaughterhouses. The large stone building housed the park's administration. They got out of the car under the eyes of the television cameras. A man in his sixties with a military crew cut walked up to them, his stare unyielding.

"Louis Roche, chief of security for the Parc de la Villette. We'll drive to the scene. A few of my men will lead the way. The local precinct chief and Laurence Clavel, the park director, are waiting for you," the man said, climbing into the back seat.

"Don't you have camera surveillance?" Nico asked, scanning the area.

"We favor human surveillance, and that's been more than sufficient. Our stats would put the neighboring precincts to shame."

His tone was surprisingly relaxed. An old man from yesteryear, a relic, Nico thought. Maybe a former cop or a retired firefighter. Private security services had recruited from their ranks for ages. Now, however, specialized university graduates prevailed in these careers.

"The park has three to four million visitors every year," the head of security was saying. "All told, we've only had about twenty gang incidents, thirty acts of vandalism, and as many thefts. Fifty percent of the time, the criminals were caught by park agents and brought to the Pavillon Janvier, where police took them into custody."

"How many people work for you?" Michel Cohen asked as the car made its way out of the parking lot.

"Nineteen, all patrolling on foot or by car. I recruit dog handlers for the night shift and hire temporary reinforcements for bigger events like open-air movie screenings and the Bastille Day fireworks. Our role is to prevent and intervene, and we can handle first aid, fire hazards, and emergencies. For everything else, we call the police."

"You're from the force, aren't you?" Nico said.

"I stepped down as captain," Roche confirmed with a quick smile.

"So you're employed by the park and the Grand Halle de la Villette?" asked the prosecutor.

"Yes, the concessions and other businesses in the park have their own security."

They skirted around the Zénith concert arena, crossed the Canal de l'Ourcq—the "Little Venice of Paris"—and passed the Cabaret Sauvage. They also drove by several of the park's famous architectural follies, thirty-five large red sculptures in various geometric shapes.

"Some have been made into playrooms and information, ticketing, and first-aid centers. One is a restaurant, and another is a coffee shop," Roche explained. "But most are merely decorative. The director calls them hollow teeth."

Nico was reminded of Bruno Guedj, a pharmacist from a case a few months earlier. He had been clever enough to hide an incriminating note in one of his teeth.

They stopped at the edge of the Prairie du Cercle.

"The canal runs down the middle of the meadow," Roche said as he opened the car door. On both sides, the Observatoire and Belvédère follies offered a bird's-eye view of the site.

Roche brightened up. He was in his element.

They had barely stepped out of the car when the local precinct chief swooped down on them. In the distance, Nico saw a man who was hunched over. Someone was offering him water. It was the artist himself, Samuel Cassian. The prosecutor and Michel Cohen were already heading toward him, amid shouts from reporters hoping for answers to their questions.

Nico shook the precinct chief's hand.

"Glad you're here," the precinct official said without ceremony. "Let me introduce you to the general director of the park, Laurence Clavel."

The director extended her hand. "The park's president is away on a business trip," she said. "He'll get here as soon as he can."

Nico recalled that the park president had been an actor in a police show on television.

"There's no rush," Nico replied amiably. It was always best to put people at ease.

"The body's been there for quite a while," said the precinct chief. "There's nothing but bones left."

"It's revolting," Clavel said, looking away with a frown.

Nico was thinking about Samuel Cassian and his 120 dinner guests three decades earlier. The news had to be upsetting for those who were still alive.

"Has the site been cordoned off?" Nico asked. "Nobody should get near the pit."

"Of course. But we can't take too long. I don't have enough staff for that," the precinct chief said.

"We'll remedy that situation as soon as we can," Nico assured him.

They would soon know the victim's age, gender, height, and ethnicity. They would also know the cause of death and whether he or she had suffered any injuries. Forensic anthropology was a specialty of the chief medical examiner.

"If you'll excuse me, I have to speak with my team," Nico said.

Accompanied by two members of Kriven's team, Captain Franck Plassard was taking the first witness accounts, for what they were worth. Memory was fickle, and using it required the greatest vigilance. No matter how many people were in a room with a suspect, half would swear that he was wearing a black pullover, and the other half would insist that the sweater was white. Every description came from someone's subjective perception. Of course his teams all used techniques developed by psychologists, but there was still a margin of error.

Nico walked over to Pierre Vidal, who was responsible for examining the crime scene. He was putting on a sterile suit so as not to contaminate the pit. His toolbox had everything he needed to gather and preserve the evidence he'd find.

His assistant, Lieutenant Paco d'Almeida, was snapping shot after shot with his digital camera and jotting down observations in his notebook.

"You'll need some help," Nico said.

"Professor Queneau's not going to be pleased," Vidal replied. "He's about to retire, and he won't like being hit with something this big at this point."

Nico disagreed but didn't say anything. Charles Queneau had buried himself in his work—managing the police forensics lab on the Quai de l'Horlage—to ease his grief over his wife's death. He would take on this new assignment with the same drive that he had brought to every other assignment. That said, Nico thought it would do him good to spend more time with his grandchildren. They would give his life new meaning and purpose.

"I'll suggest to the prosecutor that we call in the lab experts," Nico said. The Code of Criminal Procedure outlined the rules of a preliminary investigation: the prosecutor had to authorize bringing in any new person.

In France, forensics experts rarely traveled to a crime scene. Police officers, especially those working in the criminal investigation division, were trained to collect evidence. The scientists stayed in the lab, where they used their sophisticated equipment to analyze what the cops brought in.

"Be careful!" Kriven yelled to Vidal.

Nearly unrecognizable under his hood and his protective goggles, Pierre Vidal was slipping into the pit. Witnesses were staring wide-eyed: the scene looked like something out of a horror film.

"No point in taking a pulse. He's dead," Kriven said.

The skull that had rolled across the table, its empty eye sockets peering at Nico, wasn't about to disagree.

3

The arrangement of the body, which was really nothing more than scattered bones and a few bits of mummified flesh, suggested that its owner may have been sitting at the table. A suicidal guest? The victim of an accident? Neither scenario seemed likely; it didn't take a rocket scientist to figure out that someone had played a nasty trick. The skeleton completed an eccentric vision of an eternal banquet. A macabre *mise-en-scène.*

"Not everything is where it was originally," Professor Charles Queneau said. He had joined the teams at the crime site. "The soil has shifted over the years. Visitors have been walking on the lawn. The gardeners have been doing their jobs too, and then there are moles, rabbits, rats, and such."

The forensics officers were kneeling side by side, examining the grass, collecting soil and plant samples, and looking for any seeds or pollen to compare with any trace evidence they might find on a suspect's shoes or clothes. They isolated pieces of evidence, bagged them, labeled them, and recorded them for analysis later.

In the pit, a second team had come together around Captain Vidal. The fingerprint experts were working with brushes, powders, and lasers in search of fibers, hairs, and other small biological traces—all potentially useful for DNA identification.

"They shouldn't delude themselves. The weather and the years have most likely destroyed any evidence," Queneau said.

There was little chance of obtaining interpretable results. Given the media coverage, however, having forensics officers at the scene would placate everyone.

"There's hardly anything left of the body. It has putrefied and been devoured by animals," Professor Queneau said. "Maggots, flies, and beetles have all been at work."

"What about his clothes?" Lormes asked. The prosecutor couldn't stop looking at the pit.

"They've decomposed," Queneau said. "We'll look for labels, which are more durable than the clothing itself, and they might give us a clue or a lead. But really, we don't have much to go on."

"There you are!" Michel Cohen shouted. "Samuel Cassian's just been taken to the hospital."

"For shock? Or does he have an underlying heart problem?" Lormes asked.

"The medic didn't say. He's an old man."

"Yes. This would upset even a young artist. Cassian's work has been desecrated in the most horrifying way."

The men in white began to take the bones out of the pit to inventory them. They would then put the bones in sealed bags.

"His shoes are down here too," Vidal said under his mask. "And there are a few bones inside."

"I found a watch!" one of the officers shouted. "On the victim's left radial bone."

Queneau examined it. "An invention of Frenchman Louis Cartier and Hans Wilsdorf of Germany, dating back to 1904."

"A quartz watch."

"This one hit the market at the end of the sixties, going by the model and the mechanism."

"There's a belt," Vidal said.

"Nothing says it belongs to the victim," Commander Kriven said.

"Wrap it all up for me," Nico ordered.

"And there we have it. All we need to do is find the wallet and ID, and we can confirm that we've unearthed Skeletor. Our job is done," Kriven said, trying to rouse some spirits.

Louis Roche joined them at the edge of the pit. "Ms. Clavel and Antoine Gazani, the president of the National Institute for Rescue Archaeology, are at your disposal. In case you're wondering, rescue archaeologists are experts who help developers and others, such as Mr. Cassian, preserve historic items that have been unearthed."

Michel Cohen and Lormes decided to supervise the end of the operations at the Prairie du Cercle.

Nico motioned for Kriven to follow him. They returned to their car and made a U-turn. As they drove along the isolated park road toward the Boulevards des Maréchaux and the northern beltway, the sound of highway traffic rumbled in the distance.

Roche pointed. "There's the Halle aux Cuirs. It's used for rehearsal studios and storage." Tractor-trailers and other vehicles were parked amid a variety of construction materials.

"What's that over there?" Kriven asked.

"Oh, that's just the no-man's-land between the park and the suburb of Pantin. There are always a few oddballs out there, and the beltway hasn't helped matters. In November 1999, a nineteen-year-old Bulgarian prostitute was found there, stabbed to death with twenty-three knife wounds. It wasn't a pretty sight."

Just ahead they could see a fountain with Barbary lions. It was a monument to Napoleon's Egyptian campaign. They parked behind the Pavillon Janvier. Captain Plassard had already requisitioned space in the building, and the officers had begun their interviews. Questioning would soon be moved to police headquarters, where it would go on for several days. This was a massive assembly-line-style undertaking that carried serious risks.

Crucial information could be missed. And liars loved to deceive police officers. Nico, Kriven, and Roche walked through the security offices, giving Plassard and the other squad members a nod, and took the elevator to the third floor. Roche knocked on the general director's door and opened it. He ushered Nico and Kriven in and left without a word.

The park and other officials, arrayed on a comfortable sofa, got up to welcome them. The décor was modern. Along one wall, bookshelves were lined with beautifully bound volumes. A framed map of the Parc de la Villette had been laid out on the floor.

"Can I offer you something?" Clavel asked.

"I'm good, thank you," Nico said.

They sat down. Kriven took out his notebook and pen.

"Let's start at the beginning, if that suits you."

"Of course. A bit after one o'clock—"

"No, that's not what I meant," Nico said. "Let's start with the park." He pointed to the map.

The director, an energetic woman, seemed nervous and unsure of what he wanted. Nico wanted to get a sense of the place. Maybe it would help him understand why Samuel Cassian had chosen it as the burial site for his final banquet.

"Tell me about La Villette," he said.

She lit up and seemed to forget the reason for their meeting.

"This place is a city within the city. It's an incredible story…"

4

"The park is seeping with history," Clavel rhapsodized. "La Villette—which means *la petite ville*, the little city—was once the site of a Gallo-Roman village. It was a fertile area where people made their living on the land. It was also the site of the Montfaucon gallows, which were built to render King Louis IX's verdicts in the thirteenth century."

Kriven grimaced and looked entirely focused on every word the woman was saying. Nico figured he was visualizing the dead men hanging from their ropes, their skin giving off a pestilential odor as they dangled over the pit beneath the scaffold.

"It was at La Villette that Baron Haussmann decided to create a single location for Paris's animal markets and slaughterhouses, which Napoleon III inaugurated in 1867. La Villette became the Cité du Sang, the City of Blood."

Cows stabbed in the forehead, calves and lambs slit across the throat, pigs bled dry before being roasted, animals hung from metal hooks and carved up—sights and smells as nauseating as those of the Montfaucon gallows. Now the images were flowing through Nico's overactive brain.

"Even today, 'La Villette' is the name given to a thick and bloody cut of beef served in many Parisian restaurants."

"Interesting," Nico said. He was still managing to keep a smile pasted on his face. The director continued.

"Faced with the rapid growth of the meat and re-frigeration industries at the beginning of the twentieth century, the question of modernizing the abattoirs was raised, and finally, in 1958, Paris's municipal council voted to rebuild them. It was a catastrophe. The project went over budget and ended up costing several billion francs. It was considered the greatest financial scandal of the Fifth Republic."

"If memory serves me, 1974 was when the last cow was slaughtered here, and they finally closed the abattoirs," Nico said.

"That's right. The area became a wasteland—a hundred and thirty-six acres in the heart of a working-class area. Converting the acreage to leisure, cultural, and recreational use with a museum of science, technology, and industry was first proposed during Giscard d'Estaing's presidency. The Cité de la Musique was added to the plan later. Then, during Francois Miterrand's presidency, an international competition to find an architect for the park was held. Mitterrand was the one who finally brought the capital's first urban park to fruition. La Villette becoming one of the city's cultural highlights was really a kind of accident: it began as just a way to recycle an abandoned piece of land."

Nico was intrigued. "André Breton had this saying that I love. 'The accidents of work are far more beautiful than marriages of convenience.'"

"Indeed, Chief, it is a fitting quote," Clavel said. She continued without missing a beat. "La Villette is a perfect example of a beautiful accident. Several projects have garnered acclaim: the Zénith, the Cité des Sciences, the Cité de la Musique, and the Poney Club—a private initiative. By some kind of magic, Bernard Tschumi, the park's architect, was able to pull together this collection of eclectic creations."

"How did he do it?" Nico asked.

"By laying out the park in a system of points and lines. The architectural follies—those red structures—give rhythm to the park and offer visitors places where they can relax and take in the view. As for the lines, they allow you to cross the park from east to west and from north to south. The promenade takes you around the whole park, twisting like a strip of film tossed on the ground. By following the promenade, you can see the twelve gardens. The park also has two tree-lined prairies, as well as bee-hives, grapevines, and a French church garden."

"And the 'marriages of convenience'?" Nico asked, despite himself.

"The conservatory and the museum, for example, combine to make the Cité de la Musique. And there's the Philharmonie de Paris with its fantastic concert hall."

"So it was in this park that Samuel Cassian decided to bury his life-sized *tableau-piège*?" Nico said.

"Yes, Cassian was an exceptionally famous artist. And when he decided to bury his final 'banquet-perfor-mance'—which is the appropriate term—thirty years ago, the government saw a unique opportunity to raise the park's profile even higher, both culturally and scientifically."

"Why the Prairie du Cercle?" Nico asked.

"The story goes that Samuel Cassian met with Tschumi and Jacques Langier, the minister of culture. Two sites were suggested. To the south were the buildings paying homage to the former market where animals were fawned over and auctioned off, and to the north, near the Géode and the Cité des Sciences et de l'Industrie, next to the abattoirs, was where animals were slaugh-tered. This was the dangerous world of the butchers, who were nicknamed the murderers of La Villette."

The room went quiet. Nico was thinking about Cassian's decision. He imagined him putting a decisive finger on the map.

Nico turned to Gazani, who was also a university professor and director of an archaeological lab at the National Center for Scientific Research.

"Is that when the National Institute of Rescue Archaeology came in?" he asked.

"Not exactly," the man replied quietly. "Our organization didn't exist before 2002."

"What's rescue archaeology?" Kriven asked.

"Some archaeologists focus on preserving and protecting sites crucial to our heritage. In France, this area of archaeology took hold in 1997, in Rodez, when a developer caused a scandal by destroying some Roman ruins. These days, when a developer happens upon a significant site during planning or construction, rescue archaeologists are called in to make sure the site and its artifacts are protected. You probably don't know this, but there's something of interest along any highway in France, and every couple of acres, there's a one in four chance of discovering something."

"Are you saying the institute wasn't involved in Cassian's project from the start?" Nico asked.

"No, it was the archaeological department of the City of Paris. They immediately understood that this would be the first excavation of modern art. It was an unprecedented opportunity. And when disinterment came around, I wanted the institute involved at all costs."

"Why was it so important for you?"

"We wanted to find out what remained of this banquet after three decades. Then we could measure the discrepancy between memory and reality. Of the 120 attendees, several claimed that the pit was parallel to the Canal de l'Ourcq, while others insisted that it was perpendicular. Several recalled wooden tables; others, plastic. There wasn't even a consensus on who attended. This just goes to show you how fallible memories can be. But you probably know that all too well, considering your line of work."

The archaeologist seemed to enjoy having a captive audience and went on. "There was also the sociological angle. Did you know that there's an archaeology of banquets? Gallic banquets, for example, are my specialty. This project would allow us to consider the customs and table manners of the eighties' artistic elite. Every guest at this banquet had to bring his own silverware and other personal items, understanding that they would traverse several decades. In the end, most of them came with camping utensils and items from flea markets. We even found a used toothbrush."

"Along with a body," Kriven interjected.

Everyone turned and looked at him.

"Yes, well, there was that, wasn't there?" the archaeologist said, clearing his throat. "A quite unexpected find."

Seeing that Kriven had put the man on the defensive, Nico intervened. "Go on, professor. Anything about the banquet could be a lead or help us identify the body found in the pit."

"Despite their crude utensils, these guests were well-mannered. They arranged their forks and knives correctly on the plate when they were done eating. And the scraps help us understand human society. We call it garbage archaeology. The new realists stole the idea. They focused on everyday objects and their future. Samuel Cassian was one of these artists. He was intensely aware of ecology and the massive waste of our consumerist society. César Baldaccini, with his crushed cars, also comes to mind. Ultimately, the whole experience raises another question: Can an artist's approach and technique survive beyond their time?"

"I understand that he wanted to end that artistic chapter in his life. Do you know if he had a personal reason for burying this final banquet?" Nico asked.

"Some sociologists have claimed that it was about burying the illusions of the once-trendy Left. Relations between François Mitterrand and the artistic milieu, which he supported in the very early eighties, had turned chilly. His campaign promises were wiped out by austerity measures. The franc kept on being devalued, and the Socialist party was declining in the polls. As for me, I haven't made up my mind. Cassian has talked about his father's slaying. He was a Romanian Jew who was gunned down by the Nazis when Cassian was a child and tossed into a long pit similar to the one he dug in the Prairie du Cercle. But can we ever really know an artist's motivations?"

"He might not be fully aware of them himself," Nico said. "Who's in charge of the dig?"

"The Society for the Disinterment of the *Tableau-Piège*, created by Samuel Cassian," said Clavel. "It's an interdisciplinary group of archaeologists, ethnologists, anthropologists, artists, writers, filmmakers, and journalists. The University of Paris, the Ecole des Hautes Etudes en Sciences Sociales, the National Center for Scientific Research, and"—she gestured toward Gazani—"the institute are all involved."

"The tables were buried in a trench five feet deep and 130 feet long," the archaeologist said. "Thirty feet or so have been exhumed so far."

"How did you pick that portion?" Nico asked.

"The Society for the Disinterment of the *Tableau-Piège* stipulated in writing that the work should begin on the side where Samuel Cassian and fellow artist Niki de Saint Phalle were seated."

"I imagine you have a seating chart."

"No, we have only the menu: an appetizer buffet followed by giblets and exotic dishes such as tripe sausage and pig's breast, ears, tails, and feet; python ragout; and elephant-trunk steak."

"And everybody could stomach that?" Kriven asked.

"It suited some people's taste more than others," Gazani said with a smile that looked half amused and half blasé. "The seating chart was reconstructed, based on testimony. Of course, it's not definitively accurate. But we have pictures."

"We'll need to see them," Nico said.

"The park archivist has a complete set," said Clavel.

"Please have that person come to headquarters tomorrow morning with printouts for Commander Kriven."

"This… this incident is a terrible blow for the park."

"I'm sure it will attract even more visitors to La Villette," Kriven replied.

The woman glared at him.

"Okay, I think we're done for today," Nico said, trying to nip any confrontation before it could escalate. "I have no doubt that we'll be meeting again soon."

He got up, as did Kriven and everyone else. Clavel escorted them back to the front of the Pavillon Janvier. Outside, multicolored lights gave the grounds and buildings a festive look. It was almost like being on an immense futuristic vessel—perhaps the USS Enterprise— about to embark on an intergalactic voyage.

Nico's cell phone rang, interrupting his Star Trek fantasy. It was Deputy Chief Claire Le Marec, his right hand. "You're on the eight o'clock news."

"Wonderful. I can't wait to hear what they're saying now."

"They're all over the City of Blood. Is that what they really called those old slaughterhouses?" Le Marec asked.

"Indeed, that's what they were called," Nico said.

It hadn't escaped his notice that Samuel Cassian had decided to bury his banquet north of the Canal de l'Ourcq. Homage, no doubt, to the animals sacrificed and then consumed and to the butchers who had slit the animals' throats with their razor-sharp knives before stripping them of their hides. Homage to hell.

Cassian had played with fire and awakened the devil.

5

The night was relentless. An army of furious skeletons brandishing knives and forks pursued him across the Parc de la Villette, which had become a labyrinth of dead ends. Nico woke up in a cold sweat, curled in Caroline's arms. A kiss was somehow enough to ease his fears.

It was the morning of a new day, but it was starting as unpleasantly as his nightmares had ended. The morgue, in an austere redbrick structure on the Quai de la Rapée, was wedged between the Seine and the aboveground métro tracks. Nico climbed the neoclassical steps to the building that housed the medical examiner's office. More than three thousand autopsies were performed every year in this twenty-thousand-square-foot building. Professor Armelle Vilars ruled here with equanimity. As the chief medical examiner, she was frequently an expert witness at trials and was renowned both in France and abroad. She had even been called to Rwanda and Kosovo. Vilars intimidated a lot of people, but not Nico. On the contrary, this singular woman astonished him, and not just because she knew how to hold her own in a man's world.

The guard saluted Nico with a respectful "sir." Pierre Vidal was waiting for him, and the two men went into the locker room.

"You're looking good," Nico said as he took off his vest and tie. It was always too warm in the autopsy rooms.

"I stopped smoking."

They put on smocks and went to the washroom to scrub their hands.

"This is going to be a piece of cake," Vidal said. "No incisions, no cut-up organs, no blood. There won't be any smell. What could be more pleasant?"

A morgue attendant told them that Professor Vilars was ready. His French title, *agent d'amphithéâtre*, was an amusing one for someone whose job was preparing bodies for autopsy. The term was a reference to the rooms in old medical schools that had labs all around.

Edmond About, a nineteenth-century academic and satirist, had made light of autopsies. He explained them this way: "You will be thrown on a stone table, your body will be cut in pieces. One saw-bones will cleave off your great stupid head with a hatchet." Unlike Edmond About, Armelle Vilars had a reverence for the dead and their families.

The attendant accompanied them to the autopsy room, with its stainless-steel tables edged with drains and its sinks and faucets along the wall. An old man was waiting, stretched out for eternity. His legs were covered with livor mortis, purple splotches where blood had accumulated. His eyes were taped shut. Nico knew this was done to keep the corneas from drying out. Perhaps the man's would be harvested for transplanting. Corneas could be donated as much as seventy-two hours after death. A box was next to the cadaver. On the plastic cover, someone had written "autopsy room" in felt marker. The box contained the examiner's sterilized tools: round-tip scissors for cutting the aorta and ligaments; dissection scissors; a thick scalpel for cutting through cartilage; a large knife for amputations; tongs; a ladle for emptying the belly's contents; a hammer to break the skull; and needles to stitch everything back up. It was best to forget about eating before watching an autopsy and to remember that this was a human being. Deceased, perhaps, but still human.

The bones that had been numbered and arranged on another table were less unnerving than this unfortunate old man. Lormes, the public prosecutor, had turned them over. The medical examiner's office—"Professor Vilars and her orchestra," as Magistrate Alexandre Becker liked to joke—never got involved unless the public prosecutor's office asked. But the majority of the prosecutors asked to be excused from the autopsies they ordered, claiming lack of time. They relied on the police officers, who were required to attend. Nico didn't harbor any resentment in this regard. Dealing with the dead was no easy matter, and he knew the morgue inspired disgust and fear.

For strength, Nico summoned up the mental image of Caroline's face, her dark eyes and deep gaze and her charming smile. Dr. Caroline Dalry, head of gastroenterology at the Saint-Antoine Hospital, was the woman in his life. He'd known it at first sight. As much as he loved his job, he couldn't stand it when his work kept them apart for a night. And his son, Dimitri, had also taken to her immediately.

"I've allowed two medical students to watch this autopsy," Professor Vilars said. She was already concentrating. "Forensic anthropology is not a very large field, and this specific case will benefit them."

Nico nodded at the students, who looked tense and scared.

"I told them that the police chief would be here. They're undoubtedly impressed," Vilars said calmly. "That said, they're bound by confidentiality, and I'm very firm about that."

Everything was ready for the chief medical examiner. She put on a waterproof green apron over her scrubs, slipped her hair under a cap, and pulled on surgical gloves. She tied on her mask and turned on the digital recorder.

"First off, we have human bones on the table. Our goal is to determine the age, sex, height, and ethnicity of the subject. We will attempt to figure out the person's medical history and establish the date and cause of death and whether the deceased was linked to a crime. Bones have much to tell us. We just have to listen. Let's first try to determine the age. For that, we need to examine the development and aging of specific bones. Any ideas?"

"There aren't any signs of arthritis," said one of the students. "No vertebral osteophytes."

"That's correct. There are no signs of the musculoskeletal degeneration we'd see in an older person. Anything else?"

"Conversely, the bones are dense and thick, so ossification is complete," the young woman said.

"That's right. And look here. The inferior epiphysis of the radius has fused with the radial shaft."

"The epi-what?" asked Captain Vidal.

The students gave the police officer a worried look. Nico held back a smile. They were probably wondering if Vidal was trying to trick them.

"The ends of a long bone develop separately from the main part when a human is growing and fuse in adulthood," said the chief medical examiner. "In terms of the radius, fusion happens at age seventeen for men and at age twenty for women."

She took a fragment of the humerus and began to slice it. A few steps away, coroners had set out their instruments at the old man's table. One of them opened the thorax and the abdomen with a vertical incision from the xyphoid process to the pubis. It was an unappetizing spectacle. The other one took the tape off the cadaver's right eye, sprayed it with antiseptic, stretched a surgical drape with a hole over the eye, and reached for a scalpel. So the man's corneas would, in fact, be transplanted.

"Now I'm going to soak the bony structure with Nile blue. The older the subject is, the more vivid the blue will be."

All eyes were on Professor Vilars.

"We can conclude that the subject was between sixteen and thirty at the time of death. Let's turn to gender now. How can we tell the difference?"

"With the skull and the pelvis," said the female student.

"Do explain."

"Two regions should be taken into consideration with the skull: the brow bone and the occipital protuberance. Both are more prominent in men. The pelvis is lower and larger in women."

"Which is the more definitive of the two: the skull or the pelvis?"

"The pelvis."

"It's also possible to see if a woman has given birth," the student said.

"In our case, what do you see?"

"The sacrum and the aperture are both typical of a man, I would say."

"Correct. The skeleton, normally composed of 206 bones, is incomplete here, but we can use a femur, which will help us estimate the height of the individual. Which equation should we use?

"People are about 2.6 times taller than the length of their femurs," exclaimed the student. She looked ready to press the buzzer on a game show.

Vilars took out a measuring tape and unrolled it along the thigh bone.

"Twenty-six inches, so approximately five and a half feet. Let's recap. Here we have a man between seventeen and thirty years old and about five and a half feet tall. Now let's look at the question of his ethnicity, although we can't be precise on that matter."

"The shape of his skull suggests that the subject is Caucasian," said the student.

"That was a term introduced by the anthropologist Johann Friedrich Blumenbach, who considered Georgians the world's most beautiful humans and the

Caucasus, where they came from, the cradle of humanity," Vilars said.

Nico's thoughts turned to Georgia, bordered by Ukraine and Russia: three states touching the Black Sea. The video of his family's trip to what was once called the tsar's attic filled his mind: Kiev, the Carpathians, the Dniester Canyon, Odessa, and the coast of the Black Sea. They had flown home from Moscow a few weeks earlier. For the rest of their lives, they would have memories of the land of their ancestors. Walking up the Potemkin Stairs, his mother, Anya, had declared: "I've seen Odessa. Now I can die!" That was Anya: a drama queen in the true Slavic tradition. She was an indomitable woman who loved caviar and iced vodka and was fascinated by Griboyedov, Pushkin, Lermontov, and Gogol.

"Caucasian skulls are usually high and large. The cheekbones and jaw are prominent, and the chin often curves back," Vilars continued. "That's what we're seeing here, without any question. We'll still have to proceed with complementary analyses."

"We recovered a metal rod and several screws, about as long as a leg bone," Nico said.

Vilars opened the evidence bag and took out the items, which she set on the table.

"It's part of a surgical brace that keeps a broken bone in place while it knits. Considering the length and diameter of this stainless-steel rod, I'd lean toward a tibia fracture."

"Can it be traced?" Vidal asked.

Vilars examined the rod. "I only see the manufacturer's name. Nothing else. That was typical at the time of the banquet."

"And can you tell us when this person died?" Nico asked.

Vidal had filled several pages in his notebook. The victim's description was taking shape.

"Determining the date of death is key to many investigations," Vilars told her students.

"At the crime scene, I'm the one who figures that out," said Vidal. "I use an electronic thermocouple thermometer that's much more precise than a medical thermometer. It has soft and rigid probes that penetrate four to six inches into the rectum. But we're counting on you, because Skeletor here doesn't have an anus."

The students burst out laughing, while Professor Vilars glared at him.

"When it comes to bones, several physical, chemical, and histological methods allow us to determine their age," the medical examiner said. "Under ultraviolet light, the bone's fluorescence diminishes from the edges to the center, depending on the age. After a century, this fluorescence is no longer present."

Vilars leaned over the skeleton with the lamp.

"Can one of you tell me about the principle of ultraviolet fluorescence?"

The male student wiped his forehead. He clearly could not remember the specifics.

"And you?" Professor Vilars asked, looking at the other student.

"When there's been electromagnetic excitation—ultraviolet light being what we use the most—specific molecules emit photons during their de-excitation."

"There's still some activity, so we can deduce that the subject is contemporary. From there, we'll look for other indicators. Fat disappears in the spongy bone about ten years after death; proteins don't last for more than five years; the quantity of nitrogen and amino acids declines. All this, of course, depends entirely on where the body lay."

In a whirl of activity, Vilars took bone samples and set them on slides, handled mysterious liquids, and invited the students to look through the microscope.

"Anthropology has one last method," the chief medical examiner said. "Carbon-14 dating. Carbon-14 is radioactive and has a specific half-life. This allows us to determine the length of time since death. The method is particularly interesting, because carbon content is not dependent on environmental conditions. The only problem is that the preparation takes a long time, so I will have to take care of that later. Still, the initial findings suggest that this subject has been dead for twenty-five to thirty-five years. I will confirm it in my final report."

Vilars gave Nico an emphatic nod. He understood what she was saying: if this was a homicide, the statute of limitations could be an issue. In principle, prosecutions were discouraged ten years after a crime, as it was believed that the risk of judicial error increased over time. Nonetheless, magistrates used all sorts of legal tricks to get around this time limit. Moreover, the statute of limitations did not affect the opening of an investigation, which, if it focused on finding the truth rather than pursuing the suspect, could provide answers for the victim's family. Sometimes this type of investigation could even yield an arrest. So the machine had been set in motion. Nico returned the professor's nod with one of his own.

"Now we have to look for bone characteristics that are normal, pathological, or taphonomic," the professor said. "Do either of you know what taphonomic means?"

"The totality of factors that alter the morphology of bones after a subject's death," said the male student.

"Exactly right. To be specific, this subject, who was rather young, was clearly in good health. No signs of malnutrition, arthritis, or cancer—which would damage the bone structure. The lesions we see here correspond to taphonomic degradation of skeletal tissue by scavenging insects. Now let's examine the skull."

Nico looked at the skull resting on the stainless-steel table. Its sockets seemed to be staring at him. The curve of its jaw suggested perpetual laughter. If Skeletor were auditioning for a horror film, he'd get a role.

"There aren't any cranial sutures. The alveolar bone is in good shape, and the teeth are relatively undamaged. These indicators bring the likely age down to twenty to twenty-five years."

Vilars closed the jaw, and the skull was sniggering again.

"Once you think you know who this skeleton belongs to, we'll compare it with his dental records and medical history to confirm the identity. The tibia fracture helps. In the meantime, I'll send the skull to the police forensics lab, which will reconstruct his face on the computer."

The room fell silent. The medical examiner examined the skull gently and attentively.

"There's a fracture around the right parietal and temporal areas, just as Captain Vidal noted in his preliminary observations," she said.

"The body has been buried for more than twenty-five years and not in a cemetery. It appears to be a criminal act."

"The fracture was caused by blunt-force trauma," Vilars confirmed.

"A blow that could have killed him?" Nico asked.

The students watched wordlessly. It was a scene out of the movies: a summit between Paris's foremost medical examiner and the chief of the famous Criminal Investigative Division at 36 Quai des Orfévres.

"The nature of the impact, the diameter of the fracture, and its shape all correspond with a blow from a hammer. The force alone would be enough to cause cranial trauma, with loss of consciousness or an immediate coma, followed by a cerebral edema and an intracranial hemorrhage. He died within an hour."

Nico imagined the scene in slow motion, the body collapsing, the man dying.

"Life is a difficult exercise that always ends badly," Vilars told her students. "I see the proof every day."

Worse for some than for others, Nico thought. He had a responsibility to apprehend the criminal or criminals who had brutally murdered this young man and buried him in the Parc de la Villette. While he admired people like Caroline, who dedicated their lives to fighting sickness, there had to be others like him, who ensured that society did not descend to a chaos where men were free to maim and murder, and survivors were free to carry out their own brand of justice.

"I'll take DNA from the tissue remains," Vilars said. The police lab will analyze the samples. I won't detain you any longer. It's already late in the morning. I'll send the public prosecutor the report this afternoon."

"Can you send me a copy?" Nico asked. They were close colleagues who didn't need to observe all of the administrative formalities.

"Of course. I'll e-mail it to you."

Nico and Kriven, relieved to be done, quickly left the autopsy room without looking at the gutted old man. They returned to the locker room to change and head back to work.

Nico took his phone out. Vilars would not tolerate any cell phone calls in the autopsy room. There was a text message from Kriven: "I think I know who Skeletor is."

6

She poked her head out the window and breathed the springtime air: a mixture of flowers, exhaust fumes, and food. The smells of Paris. Even the nauseating ones invigorated her. She took in the view from her sixth-floor apartment. The best view of the capital, she thought. She would never give it up. She liked to sit behind the window or on her narrow balcony, a book in her hand, her eyes moving from the yellowed pages to the majestic edifice at the end of the street. "I am the light of the world: he that followeth me shall not walk in darkness, but shall have the light of life," she recited to herself. Her eyes filled with tears. It was such a beautiful day. Her voice rose. "I am the door: by me if any man enter in, he shall be saved, and shall go in and out, and find pasture."

Something was bothering her, but she couldn't say exactly what it was.

Nico waited until all his troops had taken their places around the long table in his office. Deputy Chief Clare Le Marec was sitting to his right. He valued her work, her loyalty, and her discretion. Also seated at the table were Deputy Chief Jean-Marie Rost, one of the four section chiefs in La Crim'; Commander David Kriven, a worrier and perfectionist, as well as something of a braggart; and Captains Franck Plassard and Pierre Vidal.

"Okay, we've got our work cut out," Nico said as everybody quieted down. "The excavation involved an array of people who clearly didn't expect to find a skeleton, let alone have it covered on the news. Everybody's eyes are on us now."

"According to the autopsy, the bones belong to a white man between twenty and twenty-five years old and about five and a half feet tall," Captain Vidal said. "He had a broken tibia that required an operation and was buried for three decades. He's had a blunt blow to the skull, which most likely resulted in a cerebral edema, an intracranial hemorrhage, and then death."

"And who exactly was it that died?" Nico asked. It was Kriven's turn to talk.

She walked along the Boulevard des Courcelles toward the Place des Ternes, where she had lived for years. She loved buying flowers. Roses were her favorite, while sunflowers symbolized the warmth of summer. Snowball trees blossomed with white flowers in the springtime, and their small clusters of blood-red berries welcomed birds to her balcony in the winter. The men in the green stalls waved to her as though she were royalty. The theater kiosk, where she often bought tickets on a whim, and the antique métro entrance added to the charm of the bustling market at the end of the Rue du Faubourg Saint-Honoré. She could see the Arc de Triomphe in the heart of the eighth arrondissement.

But today nothing could distract her from the mute fear that had gripped her from the moment she woke up. Something terrible was going to happen. She was sure of it. She looked around anxiously, not knowing whether the threat was human or not.

"I've been looking into the main players for this *tableau piège* in La Villette, and I came across some interesting information," Kriven said. "It seems that Samuel Cassian has been cursed by the gods, or at least he's paid dearly for his success. First off, he lost his father during the war. Then his son disappeared a week after the banquet burial. He never surfaced again, despite an exhaustive attempt to find him."

"Which gives us reason to believe that Skeletor might be the king's son," Nico said.

La Lorraine was one of her favorite places to eat. The restaurant had the best raw bar in Paris, and she loved the oysters more than anything else.

Inside, the décor recalled a transatlantic liner, and a wide assortment of guests rubbed shoulders amid the refracted light of St.-Louis glassware. She liked this sophisticated atmosphere. Maybe it would allay her fears.

"Nataliya!" the maître d' said, holding out his arms.

He could have hugged her, but knew better.

"Your usual table?"

"But of course, Roger."

She always sat along the glass wall overlooking the crowds on the sunlight-bathed Place des Ternes. It was her ritual. She glanced at her neighbors. They looked like honest people with no dark secrets. Peril might be imminent, but it would not be at the hands of these innocent diners. Still, the lump in her throat wouldn't go down. Her hands were trembling imperceptibly, her stomach was leaden, and she was sweating.

She considered calling in reinforcements. Weren't there options in circumstances such as this: rally the troops? *Nyet*, she was too proud for that.

"Today's oysters are fresher than fresh. I'd be surprised if they weren't plucked out of the mud minutes ago," Roger whispered in her ear.

She suspected that Roger was in love with her and had been from the instant he'd first laid eyes on her. He was quivering.

"May I serve you a dozen of our finest? With a glass of white wine?"

She nodded and smiled, unable to speak.

"Nothing but the best for you!" he said before making an about-face and walking off.

Finally, she set one of her books on the table. She'd been gripping it so hard, her hands hurt. But right now she would not read, not one word. She was too worried, too busy surveying her surroundings. Someone or something was coming for her. She knew it.

"Jean-Baptiste Cassian was twenty-two years old then," Kriven said.

"What do you know about this young man?" Nico asked.

"Not much yet. He was an artist too, with a degree from the École Nationale des Beaux-Arts. He was starting to make a name for himself. He had an exhibit in New York when he disappeared. And his pieces were selling rather well."

Kriven set a few photos on the table. "I met with the archivist at the Parc de la Villette this morning. She gave me these old prints; they were taken during the banquet."

He pointed to one of the pictures.

"Here's Jean-Baptiste, sitting on his father's right."

"Well, if that isn't symbolic," Jean-Marie Rost said.

"And that's exactly where we found the body—right where Cassian's son was sitting," Nico added.

"Indeed!" Kriven said.

"All the same, we'll need to verify the victim's identity before going any further with this lead."

"We have these shoes, a clothing label, some tissue samples, a belt, and a watch," Pierre Vidal said. "They'll be examined at the lab."

"And fingerprints?" Nico asked.

"That would be a surprise. We've found these things and remnants of food near the skeleton, but I wouldn't hold my breath. A lot of time has passed."

"What about soil samples?"

"We have experts working on that, but we don't have much there, either. Let's see if Jean-Baptiste had surgery for a broken tibia. And the forensics lab is reconstructing a face from the skull. That should be interesting."

"DNA and dental records would help," Jean-Marie Rost said.

"Those are things we need to do right away," Nico said. "Have you made a list of who was at the banquet?"

"We've started putting together information from the archivist's photos," Kriven said. "And we've sent out investigators. It was an extraordinary group: artists, gallery owners, art critics, filmmakers, museum directors, journalists, politicians. A few have died. Others have retired, but the majority are still working. We're trying to find out if they noticed anything in particular about the two Cassians. Speaking of which…"

"Yes?" Nico said.

"Jacques Langier was the minister of culture back then, and he was at the lunch. How would we get in touch with him?"

"I'll do it. It won't take me long."

"And what about Cassian?"

"Go to his place now, and see if you can find any DNA traces and the dental records for his son. And talk to the boy's mother. I'll meet with Cassian later. He's been in the hospital. Do you know who was present when the excavation started?"

"We have an official list. We also have a list of everyone who has worked at the site since the dig began, as well as those who came for other reasons—park employees, journalists, and such. We can narrow the list to the people who were there when the skeleton was discovered. Murderers often return to the scene of the crime. All in all, we could fill a conference hall with the people who've been at the site, so we have our work cut out for us."

"In the meantime, I'm going to ask Christine Lormes to have the banquet completely exhumed," Nico said.

Everyone at the table gave him their full attention.

"We'll need to make sure there aren't any other nasty surprises. We're already dealing with what looks like a premeditated murder."

"You're right," Claire Le Marec said.

"Jean-Marie, will you write the preliminary report?"

"Yes, Chief."

She had barely touched her oysters or pressed her lips to the glass of white wine. The bread basket and butter dish hadn't been moved. She had no appetite. Neither the crowd beyond the window in the Place des Ternes nor the hubbub in the restaurant could help. The sky no longer seemed blue, and the sun didn't seem to be shining.

"Is something wrong?" Roger asked.

She jumped at his unexpected presence. She could see the concern on his face.

"I'll bring you six more if you're unhappy with these," the maître d' said.

She cursed herself for being an idiot. Showing this much nervousness would attract unwanted attention.

"Don't fall all over yourself," she said, teasing him. "I guess I don't have a taste for oysters today. I'd rather have the *sole meunière*. That should bring back my appetite. And I might just have one of those wonderful Grand Marnier soufflés for dessert."

He still looked worried. She was avoiding him, and that wasn't like her. She knew she had hurt his feelings.

Roger cautiously took away the oyster platter and its pedestal.

"I'll bring your sole right away."

What did her eyes take in at that moment—the last moment? Her heart was beating violently. She was beginning to sweat. There was a buzzing in her head. It was growing louder, boring into her eardrums. Through the din, she heard someone shout. It was the maître d', Roger. He was shrieking her name: "Nataliya!" Then Roger's voice went quiet. The space inside her brain exploded, throwing out thousands of brilliant shards. Then darkness.

"We need to figure out very quickly whether the skeleton is, indeed, Jean-Baptiste Cassian's," Nico said. "But the odds of finding his murderer after three decades are pretty slim, assuming he's still alive."

Nico's phone interrupted the discussion. His secretary was under orders not to bother him unless it was an emergency. Nico hurried to his desk to answer.

"Hello?"

"I think you want to take this call, Chief." His secretary sounded upset.

She put him through without waiting for approval.

"Chief Nico Sirsky?"

"Speaking."

"I'm Dr. Paul-Henri Fursac at Bichat Hospital."

Nico saw the hospital in his mind. It was in the eighteenth arrondissement on the north side of Paris.

"Your mother's been admitted."

"Wait, what happened?"

"I'd rather not discuss this with you on the phone. It would be best if you came in."

"Is she okay?"

"Listen, you should come in as soon as possible, and we can explain."

7

Nico had given his instructions and left. Commander Kriven knew from the dark look on his boss's face how urgent the situation was. The man's devotion to his mother was a well-known fact.

Mrs. Cassian looked at Kriven and Lieutenant Almeida from her place on the sofa, then blew her nose and wiped the tears from her cheeks. She was short and slim, with gray hair pulled back in a ponytail. She was clearly distraught over the events of the previous day. Her husband, Samuel, had been hospitalized for shock. Fortunately, the doctors had said he could come home soon.

"It's horrible. This project meant so much to Samuel."

Kriven tried to avoid showing his impatience.

"Ma'am, I'm sure it's a relief to know that your husband will be home in no time at all. Now, if I may, I would like to speak with you about the remains of the individual discovered at the site of the banquet."

By using the word "individual," Kriven wanted her to understand that they had, indeed, found a human being in the pit. A person with a face—at one time—and a name. It could serve as a first step. Perhaps she would make the connection between the remains and her son's disappearance. A few seconds passed without either of them breaking the silence. He had to be careful not to push too hard.

"This individual died young," Kriven prodded gently.

"That's a shame," she said quietly.

"He took a blow to the head. He didn't suffer at all."

"That's a relief."

Her mind seemed to be elsewhere, and she wasn't willing to connect the dots.

"Can you tell me about your son?"

Her eyes immediately went to the throw pillow by his knees. It had fallen off the chair when he sat down. He picked it up and propped it back in place.

"Do you remember if he ever broke his leg?"

"Jean-Baptiste," she said. A long pause followed. "We still don't know what happened to him. I'm sure he just wanted to get away from his problems. You know, he was such a promising artist, but he was upset over not being as good as his father. I think he feared disappointing him. So he left. I respect that. Maybe he's living in the United States under an assumed name. I hope he's happy. He's my son, my only child. You'll never know how much a mother can love a child."

"Tell me, ma'am, do you remember if Jean-Baptiste ever suffered any broken bones, perhaps a bone in his leg?" Kriven asked.

She glared at him, as if she couldn't bear the interruption of her idyllic reflection on parental love.

"He broke his tibia in a soccer game when he was seventeen. He gave me a good scare. His operation went well, and after his recovery, he ran as fast as a rabbit."

Kriven wasn't taking any chances.

"And how tall was he?"

"A bit shorter than you. About five feet, nine inches. But such a handsome boy."

"Have you kept his possessions?"

"Of course. I haven't moved a thing in his room."

David Kriven shivered. Underneath the success and the money, the wound was still fresh. The Cassians had continued living, but were haunted by their son's specter. People knew that Mrs. Cassian rarely went out and never saw anyone, and now he understood why: she had lost her appetite for life, along with her son.

"May I see his room?"

Mrs. Cassian was plainly suspicious. "What exactly are you looking for?"

"Well, we're hoping to find him," Kriven said. It was a lie.

The woman's eyes lit up. She got up quickly and walked across the apartment. Kriven and Lieutenant Almeida followed. As he passed the windows, Kriven took in the bustling Saint-Germain-des-Prés neighborhood. It was an artists' haunt Samuel Cassian would never leave, Kriven had found out when reading up about the man. Apparently Cassian was nostalgic for the student uprising days of the sixties, when idealistic young people would gather in the Saint Germain cafés to reenvision the world.

She had barely opened the door when Kriven understood how time had, in fact, stood still for the Cassians. A sweatshirt was still draped over the back of an armchair. The room hadn't been touched since Jean-Baptiste's disappearance. It was a mausoleum for the young man and a godsend for the police.

"May we look around?"

"Yes, but keep everything in its place."

Kriven gestured to Almeida, who opened his briefcase to begin collecting the DNA evidence necessary to make a comparison with the genetic code of the skeleton. It would take twenty-four to forty-eight hours to make that assessment.

"Did you, by any chance, keep your son's medical records?" Kriven asked.

Mrs. Cassian gave him an odd look.

"His dental records, for example."

She stared him as though he were a strange creature.

"Or at least his dentist's name?"

"Hmm, everything's in the office," she finally answered.

He followed her into the hallway. All alone in the room, Almeida could go through Jean-Baptiste's personal effects. In the office, Kriven stood in front of a desk with drawers full of folders labeled in black marker: "Middle School," "High School," "École Nationale Supérieure des Beaux-Arts," "Soccer Club," "Guitar Lessons," "Pediatrician," "General Practitioner," "Specialists," "Dentist," "Letters and Postcards," "Exhibitions." Jean-Baptiste's life had been organized, filed, and archived. Kriven gulped. The woman pulled out the dental folder, set out her son's X-rays, and looked at them with sadness on her face, as if they were beloved family photos.

"May I borrow them?" Kriven asked.

"Only if you promise you won't damage them. He may need them someday, you know."

Damn it! He'd have to ask Dominique Kreiss, the division's psychologist, to see the woman.

"You have my word," he said.

"Well, you seem like a good man, and honest, too. Like Jean-Baptiste. You'll bring them back, won't you?"

The top floor at headquarters was filled with small interview rooms. The rooms had computers with cameras to record the questioning. Each had only a skylight. This dearth of natural lighting gave the rooms a claustrophobic feel and also deterred escapes. The room Captain Franck Plassard was in felt even gloomier as he thought about his boss and Anya Sirsky.

The door opened, and an officer poked his head into the room.

"Mrs. Béal is here," he said.

The director of Monaco's contemporary art museum, the Nouveau Musée National, had attended Samuel Cassian's banquet, as well as the opening ceremony for the archaeological dig. She was a major player in the art world.

"Send her in," Plassard said.

The officer let her in, then closed the door and stood in a corner. In French cop lingo, the officer in the background was called a "ghost"—not seen, not heard, but there.

Plassard got up to greet the witness and asked her to take a seat.

"I have to thank you for responding so quickly." He wanted to set her at ease; he had no reason to consider her a suspect. At the moment, no one was a suspect.

"It's absolutely fine. This isn't a practical joke to draw more attention to the dig, is it?"

"I'm sorry to tell you that the bones we've uncovered are human remains, as we suspected."

"My God! But who could it be?"

"We haven't gotten that far yet," Plassard said in a soothing tone. "You were at the banquet and the excavation of Samuel Cassian's *tableau-piège*. Tell me: Did you notice anything in particular at either of these two events? I know the banquet took place a long time ago, but it must stand out in your memory."

"Oh, we were all so happy and excited to take part in this experience. We were all friends, some of us closer than others. We discussed ideas. We talked about the arts. And we laughed. It was a lovely event. Samuel's idea to bury his last banquet and symbolically renounce his *tableaux-pièges* was sheer genius."

The captain smiled politely.

"What else can I tell you? We had to bring our own silverware and a few things to put on the table for posterity. I came with a bouquet of flowers in a white porcelain vase. The person sitting next to me drew on the vase. And he wasn't just anybody. He was Fabrice Hyber. *The* Fabrice Hyber!"

"You don't say," Captain Plassard said. "That's quite a story. I bet you wish you had that vase on your mantel now."

"Of course. Who wouldn't? One of his artworks, *The Artery*, is in the Parc de la Villette. It's an immense pathway made of ceramic tiles. A homage to AIDS victims."

"Can you recall any particular incident that day? Maybe some kind of argument?"

"Not at all. Samuel looked like he was happy to be turning over a new leaf. He wanted to work in bronze."

"In your reports to the archaeologists, you say that the tables buried in the trench were made of wood," Plassard said. "But they were plastic. Samuel Cassian thought plastic would survive better than wood."

The woman blushed. "I was mistaken about the tables. But do you think I would have forgotten an argument?"

"I suppose it isn't easy to remember everything, even about a gathering as noteworthy as Samuel Cassian's banquet." Plassard wasn't intent on trapping her, but he needed her to recall as much as she could.

She looked equal parts annoyed and perplexed. "What I remember vividly was that we all truly enjoyed ourselves."

"Was Samuel Cassian's son there?"

"Jean-Baptiste? Of course! His father had asked him to help, and he put his heart and soul into the project. He was such a charming young man with a promising future. If he hadn't disappeared so suddenly, I'm sure he'd have become one of the best artists of his generation."

"Do you know anything about his disappearance?"

"It happened a week after the banquet was buried. Like everyone else, I was shocked. Samuel was crushed. He loved his son. I'm told that his wife lost her mind. Samuel never talked about it."

"Nobody mentioned the disappearance the day they began the excavation?"

She shook her head. "Why are we talking so much about Jean-Baptiste? Has he come back after all these years?"

She had no idea how close to the mark she was.

"Damn it!" Professor Charles Queneau never liked being the last to know. Captain Vidal had told the director of the police forensics lab that Nico's mother was in the hospital, and Queneau was angry nobody had told him sooner.

"How old is she? Barely sixty-five? Damn it. Bloody hell! Do you have any other information?"

"No," the captain said. "Not at the moment. As soon as we hear anything, we'll let you know."

"Nothing to do but hope," Queneau said.

"For now, we need to focus on the investigation. That will help to ease the chief's mind. For starters, we have to confirm the victim's identity."

Queneau led the police captain into one of the labs in the Quai de l'Horloge building. This building was as old as division headquarters. To partially compensate for the lack of space, mobile units had been set up in the courtyard. Only the pleasure of being in the Latin Quarter made the cramped conditions acceptable—and even then, only for so long.

The lab was filled with workers in white coats, as well as machines connected to computers, printers, micro-scopes, and a surprising number of flasks and test tubes. As Queneau and Vidal passed by, some of the lab techs nodded and waved and returned to their work. A young woman approached them. She was holding Skeletor's watch in a gloved hand.

"It's a Rolex Explorer II," she said. "Initially, we thought the watch was older than that. This was part of a limited-edition series sold by Tiffany & Co. in 1984. It's worth four or five thousand euros today."

"That much?" Vidal said.

The scientist put the watch in a plastic bag and sealed it. Then she brought out the shoes found in the trench with a few toe bones inside.

"Our victim was pretty cool," the young woman said. "These are Adidas mi Forum Mid black-and-white shoes for men. They're Adidas's most emblematic shoes, and they also came out in 1984. If these shoes have been buried for thirty years, that certainly shows how resistant to the elements they were."

"The toes have disintegrated, but the Adidas live on. We have the makings of a brilliant advertising concept," Vidal said, smirking.

"Considering what people find acceptable today, consumers would probably go for it," Queneau said.

"Speaking of ads, I've got one to show you," the researcher said.

She turned to the computer and clicked. Ray Charles's "Hit the Road Jack" blared from the speakers. Spotlights flashed on a tennis court, and a bare-chested man leaped over the net. Yannick Noah caught a racquet and swerved wildly to hit the ball. The C17 jeans logo was visible as the narrator repeated the name over and over.

"He's hot," she said.

"These days, he's a few years worse for the wear," Vidal said.

"I bet he's stayed in shape. But you're right. This commercial is also from 1984."

"A year after his win at the Roland-Garros," Queneau said. "I was new to my job. This woman was barely born, and you, Captain, were just old enough to be building sand castles. It really is time for me to think about retirement."

"That's if you can ever tear yourself away from this place," Vidal said with a good-natured smile.

"C17 was a popular French brand in the eighties," the young woman said. "Its ads were aimed at the fifteen-to-twenty-five-year-old market, as you can tell. The leather label and the fibers we found all match up with this design."

"The belt hasn't given us any clues," Queneau said. "But overall, the victim's wardrobe aligns with Jean-Baptiste Cassian's disappearance in the middle of the eighties."

"And what about the fingerprints and samples taken at the site?" Vidal asked.

"We're drawing a blank there," Queneau responded. "We're waiting for more. Shall we?"

They walked down a floor. Skeletor's skull had been set on a metal plate. A technician was in the process of digitizing it for 3D visualization, turning it on its axis while the laser scanner recorded its image on the computer. The computer modeled the face on the basis of the skull's shape and the bones' thickness and gave it features typical of the victim's age, build, and ethnicity.

The technician, who had been at the machine for several hours, showed them the result. After a few seconds, Vidal took the photo of Jean-Baptiste Cassian out of his briefcase and held it up to the screen.

"Looks like him," Professor Queneau said.

"No kidding. They look like brothers. Good work."

"Hello!" They heard a voice behind them and turned around. Lieutenant Almeida was there, holding some bags intended for Queneau.

"Here are the DNA samples from Jean-Baptiste Cassian's home," he said. "And I've got more. You'll never believe it: a hairbrush that's been untouched since the artist's disappearance!"

DNA extraction from hair was far easier than from bones or organs. The DNA molecules were protected by a layer of keratin, which was a malleable natural substance that formed a barrier resistant to bacteria and other invaders, even after death.

"We can make the comparison with the bone samples," Queneau said.

"So it looks like we're making some headway, Professor," Vidal responded.

Deputy Chief Jean-Marie Rost was busy writing the preliminary report, a crucial part of the investigation. He had to cover the circumstances of the corpse's discovery, explain the location and presence of clues, summarize the witness accounts, and include the complete autopsy report. With his signature as section chief, the report would be sent to the prosecutor in charge of the case. Based on the conclusions, a magistrate would almost certainly open a criminal investigation, which would give them more time. The mere discovery of human bones in a trench dug and filled thirty years earlier would likely be the deciding factor. The director of the medical examiner's office had helped. According to her, a violent blow to the head was most likely the cause of death. The magistrate owed Samuel Cassian and his wife a full explanation of their son's disappearance and death, even if the statute of limitations had passed.

The phone rang. Looking up from his computer keyboard, Jean-Marie Rost paused at the picture of his son stuck to the edge of his screen. This little boy with a round head and a smile that curved like a banana was the cutest baby in the world.

"Deputy Chief Rost? Professor Vilars would like to speak with you."

"Put her on."

"Lieutenant Almeida has sent me dental records for Jean-Baptiste Cassian," Vilars said. "I've just compared the antemortem records with the X-rays."

Oral characteristics and bone morphology were significant calling cards.

"There is no room for doubt. It's a positive ID."

This was good news for the investigation.

"I'll send a note with Lieutenant Almeida to include in your preliminary report."

"Thank you, Professor."

"Of course. Any news about Mrs. Sirsky?"

Like Vilars, who spent her days and many of her nights cutting open bodies, Rost was keenly aware of how quickly loved ones could be lost. As easily as a file folder could be dropped into a trash can.

"We're waiting to hear more," he replied quietly.

"Keep me posted."

She hung up. Rost got up from his chair, left his office, and went to knock on Claire Le Marec's door.

"Come in!" she said.

"Professor Vilars just called," he said.

Le Marec's cell phone went off.

"About the dental records…"

She hunted through her bag for the phone.

"We were right. The skeleton is Cassian's son."

"Good work," she said. She gave him a quick thumbs-up before punching in a number an holding the cell phone to her ear.

"Nico?"

8

The tower of Bichat Hospital loomed, cold and imposing, over the Porte de Saint-Ouen. Nico had rushed over a few hours earlier, a bundle of nerves. The once-familiar gnawing in his gut had been reawakened. He had already lost his father. He wanted more time—a lot more time—with his mother. She was still young and full of energy. He rebuked himself for taking her to Ukraine; she'd had the vague feeling of having come full circle in that ancestral land. The trip had jinxed them.

Nico had been taken down a long hallway with cold fluorescent lights to the intensive coronary-care unit. It felt like a hostile environment, where doctors and nurses marched with muffled steps to the beat of beeping machines. Organ failure called for sophisticated technology and close surveillance. Welcome to hell, Nico thought. Here, a patient's life could hang by a single strand. Everything could be lost in a second. What was his mother doing in such a terrible place?

"Mr. Sirsky?"

Nico froze. When was the last time he took his mother to lunch on the Île Saint-Louis, a few steps from his office? Anya loved the terrace at Le Flore en l'Île on the Quai d'Orléans and the famous Berthillon ice cream served there. The restaurant was often packed with tourists, but the views of the Seine and Notre-Dame Cathedral were astonishing

"Mr. Sirsky?"

Nico thrust his hand toward the person in the white coat. Good God, what had happened?

"I'm Dr. Fursac, head of the intensive coronary-care unit."

This was the man who had called, the bearer of bad news.

"What happened? Where's my mother?" Nico asked in a tone he didn't recognize.

"Come with me to my office, and I'll explain."

They sat down facing each other. The silence was uncomfortable. Nico's anxiety kept him from talking.

"Your mother has suffered a heart attack."

Your father will die. You need to prepare yourself.

"It happened while she was eating at La Lorraine at the Place des Ternes. Roger called an ambulance immediately. He's waiting at the entrance. He'd like to talk to you before he leaves."

Nico tried to think. Who was Roger? Why had he come to the hospital with his mother?

We're making your father comfortable. He's in no pain.

"Because it was cardiac arrest, the medics began CPR."

Right hand flat on the sternum, left hand on top. Use both arms to depress the rib cage, then release. Maintain blood flow to the brain and the rest of the body.

Oh, right! Roger was the maître d' at La Lorraine.

"They used a defibrillator to shock your mother's heart."

His vital functions have stopped. Your father is dead.

"Once the ambulance came, the medic intubated her."

Nico imagined the sirens wailing, the ambulance barreling through red lights and weaving through traffic. And his mother lying inside, unconscious, defenseless, dependant on a machine. A nightmare.

"When she arrived here, we put her on a ventilator."

She wasn't breathing on her own. Nico came back to reality.

"I have to ask, Mr. Sirsky, if your mother's affairs are in order and if she has specified any final directives, should her condition take an even more serious turn."

Tears were welling in his eyes. She was alive, but this gift could be taken away at any moment. Final directives? He had never asked, and she had never broached the subject. She probably knew that he would refuse to discuss anything related to her death.

There was a knock on the door. Dr. Fursac got up to let the visitor in. Nico turned slowly, lost in thought, and saw Caroline. He pulled her into his arms.

Caroline turned to the doctor. "What's the prognosis?"

"It depends," Dr. Fursac replied. "First, concerning any cerebral anoxia…"

"That's when the brain doesn't get enough oxygen because of cardiac arrest," Caroline explained to Nico. "There can be neurological aftereffects. Fortunately, most patients survive without any problems."

"In her case, it's too early to tell," Dr. Fursac said. "For now, your mother is asleep. We've put her in an induced coma, which is standard procedure when we have to ventilate a patient."

"She's sedated and will be kept comfortable," Caroline said.

"We'll keep her sedated for about twelve hours. Then she should wake up. If, after forty-eight hours, her neurological state is fine, we'll remove the intubation tube and transfer her to a step-down unit."

Caroline nodded.

"The other issue is her ventricular fibrillation," Dr. Fursac said. "We'll have to determine the cause of this attack."

"But we're not there yet," Caroline said to Nico. "We need to be optimistic, and take this one step at a time.

Every hour that Anya remains stable will give us a bit more hope."

"I understand," Nico said. "Can I see her?"

"Your mother is unconscious, and she won't know that you're there," Dr. Fursac said. "We'll have to keep it brief."

"I'd like that, please."

"First, can you tell me who her primary-care physician is? I need to contact him."

"Umm, yes," Nico stammered. "Dr. Alexis Perrin. He's on the Rue Soufflot in the fifth arrondissement. He's my brother-in-law. What do you need from him?"

"Dr. Fursac needs to know if Anya's had any recurring problems with tachycardia," Caroline said.

"He'd have told us," Nico said.

"Not without her consent, honey. Even if he's part of the family, he's still bound by confidentiality."

"Shall we go in?" Dr. Fursac asked.

They walked down the long, narrow hallway, brushing past white walls covered with posters of landscapes. Were these images of mountains and lakes supposed to relieve visitors' stress? If so, Nico thought, they weren't doing the trick. Dr. Fursac took them through the double doors to the nurses' station and the patient rooms surrounding it.

"You'll have to wash your hands and wear a gown over your clothes."

"The intensive coronary-care unit is amazing," Caroline said, quickly putting on the gown. "A unit like this saves lives every day. It has the most advanced medical technology in the world. We should be thankful that Anya made it here."

As if they were floating on air, the medical staff moved from patient to patient, checking the machines, taking measurements, and repositioning IV bags and tubes. Despite Caroline's reassuring presence, Nico was having a hard time controlling his distress. He felt like he was sinking into cold quicksand.

They found Anya's bed. She was barely recognizable. A central venous catheter was connected to her neck. Lines running from monitoring machines to pads attached to her chest recorded her rhythms in incomprehensible spikes and curves. She was immobile and looked almost dead. Only her rib cage moved with any regularity, pushed up and down by the ventilator. Its whooshing accompanied the beeps of the machines. Nico bit his lip.

"You can say something to her," Caroline said tenderly.

He paused to collect his thoughts. Then he whispered:

> "In bleak despair and isolation
> My days stretched on in quiet strife:
> No awe of God, no inspiration,
> No love, no tears, no sense of life.
>
> And now once more I've seen that vision:
> My soul awoke; I saw your face,
> A fleeting moment's apparition
> Of perfect beauty and of grace.
>
> My spirit soars in exaltation,
> And once again there reappears
> The awe of God...and inspiration...
> The sense of life...and love...and tears."

His mother had recited these lines by Pushkin so many times, he knew them by heart.

"Hang in there, *Maman*," Nico said.

He stroked her forehead the same way she had stroked his when he was a child.

"*Ya tebya liubliu*," he said.

They left the room and went back down the hall. In the lobby, they saw a man in a suit and black bow tie. He was nervously fidgeting with the edge of his jacket.

"You're Nataliya's son!" the man said as soon as he spotted Nico.

Nataliya? Nico looked at the man, uncomprehending.

"Sorry, that's Anya. I call her Nataliya. You know, after Gilbert Bécaud's song 'Nathalie,' because its mention of the Pushkin Café on the Red Square turning white under the snow—"

Nico just stared at him for a moment, then said, "You must be Roger. She's still alive, and it's thanks to you."

"I am so relieved that we could get her here quickly. I know you're very busy, but how is she?"

"We'll have to wait and see. I'm happy to keep you updated."

"Would you please? I'd really appreciate it."

"Nico!" He turned at the sound of his sister's voice. Tanya and Alexis were running toward him. She held out her arms. She was shaking. Her blue eyes were welling with tears, and her long blonde hair was a mess.

"She's alive, Tanya. Mama's alive."

Nico gave his brother-in-law a cold stare.

"She wouldn't let me break doctor-patient confidentiality," Alexis said. "She didn't want to worry any of you. You know how stubborn she can be. We got here as quickly as we could."

"We understand, Alex," Caroline said quickly.

Alexis and Caroline had gone to medical school together, and it was because of Alexis and Tanya that he had met Caroline.

"Tell us," Nico insisted.

"Anya came to see me shortly after we got back from our trip. She was having chest pains. I ordered several tests, including electrocardiography and an ultrasound. They came back fine. All the same, I wanted her to go to the hospital and get one of those portable machines that measures cardiac activity over a twenty-four-hour span. A Holter. Anya agreed to do it, but she canceled her appointment twice. I was so furious, I threatened to quit as her doctor so I could tell you. She finally agreed and was set to go to the hospital next week."

Alexis hung his head. Caroline put her hand on his shoulder.

"I'm scared," Tanya said. She sounded exhausted.

"I'm sorry," Nico said to Alexis. "You did nothing wrong."

"Have you told Lana and Bogdan yet?" Caroline asked.

"Not yet," said Tanya. Alexis and Tanya's children were still at school. "I just left a message for them on the kitchen counter. We'll tell them when we get home."

"I'll have to break the news to Dimitri tonight too," Nico said. "He calls his grandmother about everything. Caroline and Alexis, could you keep track of Mom's condition? You're the experts." Both doctors nodded.

"Visitors are only allowed in the evenings," Caroline said.

"I'll come tomorrow at six o'clock," Nico said.

"I'll come with you," Tanya said.

"Of course. Call me later."

Once he was back outside, Nico looked at his phone. There were several text messages from colleagues who said they were keeping Anya in their thoughts and prayers.

"Dimitri might be home by now," he said.

"I've already told him that we'll be late," Caroline said.

"I'm so glad we're all under the same roof these days. Have I thanked you today for moving in with us?"

"No, I don't think so, sweetie. But I forgive you. You thanked me yesterday. While I'm thinking of it, don't forget to call Jacqueline and André."

Ties with his former in-laws had been strained during the time Dimitri's mother, Sylvie, struggled with depression and prescription-drug dependence. But Nico had managed to mend fences with Jacqueline and Andre, and they had begun seeing Dimitri again. Sylvie, who had gone into rehab, was doing better now. She was splitting her time between Paris and Royan, where her aunt lived and where she sometimes saw Dimitri. He was dragging his feet, though, and seemed to be closer to Caroline than Sylvie. In the throes of her depression, Sylvie had neglected her son, and Dimitri had suffered for it.

"Jacqueline and Andre care about Anya," Caroline said. "And they know how much Dimitri loves his grandmother."

"Of course."

Nico opened the car door for Caroline. He walked around and got in on his side. Driving away from the hospital seemed like abandoning his mother, and he felt unease in his gut. He put his hand on Caroline's thigh, and she put her hand over his. Her touch reassured him.

Just as he was beginning to breathe normally again, the hands-free phone in the car rang.

"Nico?" It was Claire Le Marec calling for news.

He took a deep breath. "She's alive, but it's too soon to tell. Fill me in on the case."

9

At night, the Parc de la Villette was a study in contrasts. Beams of vivid lights pierced the darkness, both drawing people in and pushing them away. Mathieu was sitting on a granite cube in the middle of the Leitner Cylinder, a sound tunnel about thirty feet wide. Water flowed in ribbons along its sides, which reverberated with electro-acoustic music. The whole effect exacerbated the young man's unease and sense of isolation; there was nowhere to look but up. Mathieu shivered. He was starting to get creeped out.

He felt a hand on his neck. Someone was slowly kneading the muscles. Mathieu steeled himself. A man leaned over his face and shoved his tongue inside his mouth. Get it off right here in the Leitner Cylinder? Why not? Mathieu forced himself to control his desire. Why hurry? His companion pulled him up. He ground against his back and buttocks while licking his neck. Hot and incredibly sexy. The guy yanked his collar, uncovering his shoulder before nipping it with pleasure. He knew how to take charge. He slipped his hand under his jeans and massaged Mathieu's penis. Now Mathieu couldn't hold back.

"You little slut," the man breathed in his ear. Mathieu's blood turned cold. Being teased was one thing. Getting insulted by a stranger was another. He loved the thrill, but he wasn't into kinky.

"You thought we'd fuck and that would be it?" The man sounded angry.

The man squeezed Mathieu's penis—hard—and sank his teeth into his shoulder. Mathieu cried out in pain.

"Let me go!" he shouted.

The Leitner Cylinder felt like a prison now. He had to escape. But the aggressor's arm was wrapped around him, keeping him from moving. Mathieu felt something sharp plunge deep into his abdomen. A searing pain gripped him. The bluish lights in the cylinder began to dance. Then the fountains quieted, and their murmurings faded away. The electronic sounds were now a baleful song. He collapsed.

The last thing he saw was a man who looked sullen and disgusted. He was holding a knife.

"Mama," Mathieu moaned.

Icy darkness fell.

10

Guitar chords. The rhythmic beat of a drum. Nico sat up, startled. He had collapsed in exhaustion. His phone— Bichat Hospital! He thought of his mother's heart, and his own began beating faster. Freddie Mercury's voice resounded in the quiet room. "Another one bites the dust... Another one bites the dust." He felt a hand on his back.

"It's the ringtone for La Crim'," Caroline said. Usually, that wasn't comforting, especially at three in the morning. But in this case, a bloody crime was better than bad news about Anya. "How do you think I'm going to get along," Freddie sang, as if he could read Nico's thoughts. He picked up his phone and answered, putting an end to Freddie's vocals.

"Nico? It's Claire. I know it's not the best time."

Caroline curled against him and wrapped her arms around his belly. She kissed his neck. Nico shivered.

"It's no problem," he said.

Her breasts against his back. The stirrings of an erection.

"You would have been furious if we hadn't told you right away," Claire said uneasily.

Caroline caressed his torso slowly, then slipped her hand under the sheet and found his penis. Nico clenched his teeth.

"I'm listening, Claire. What is it?"

"There was an attack in the Parc de la Villette. I wanted you to get the news from us before reading about it in the morning paper."

The investigators were required to alert the police chief or his deputy about any crime that seemed unusual. Nico guessed that Commander Charlotte Maurin had decided to call Claire Le Marec. It could have stopped there. Except it had happened in the Parc de la Villette, where they were already investigating a suspicious death, albeit an old one.

"The security people found a body in the bamboo garden. Around two in the morning."

"What stage are you at?"

"We've started searching the area. The body hasn't been taken away. I thought you might want to see it yourself."

"I'll be there. Give me twenty minutes."

"We'll wait for you here. I'll send someone to the Pavillon Janvier to pick you up and drive you to the garden."

They ended the call. Nico turned over and stretched out alongside Caroline. He kissed her passionately as she wrapped her leg around him and grabbed his hair. He knew this gesture well, and it redoubled his excitement.

"Come," she whispered.

He licked her hard nipples and ran his hand over her thigh. Caroline arched, urging him even closer. He thrust himself into her, and at the moment of penetration, his spirit left the real world. His life was nothing more than this woman he held in his arms.

They clung to each other, their muscles taut and their breathing quick. He heard her moan against his cheek, and they peaked at the same time. Their tension finally released, they held on for another minute, drawing out their caresses.

"Get up, lazy boy," Caroline sighed. She was used to emergencies and early-morning calls. She had them in her own line of work too.

Nico took a quick shower and threw on jeans and a pullover before giving her one last kiss.

"What if I crawled back in bed just for a minute or two?" he asked.

She smiled indolently.

"Duty calls, Chief."

Nico grabbed his keys and went to the underground garage. Montparnasse Tower loomed, a faithful sentry.

Deep in the Parc de la Villette, Nico and Claire Le Marec stood over a depression nearly twenty feet deep. Within it was a tropical forest. Beams of light swung over the terrain. The police officers summoned to the site looked like an expedition group ready to trek through the dense forests of the Amazon in hopes of finding an isolated tribe. But this wasn't an expedition. It was a murder investigation. And clues were what they were seeking.

"This is the bamboo garden," Claire Le Marec said. "Shall we go down?"

They descended a staircase to a Zen universe, where the ground was covered with pebbles arranged in black and white stripes. They hugged the vine- and root-filled walls to reach the team under Charlotte Maurin's command. Nico nodded to his officers.

"It's a whole microclimate here," Le Marec said. "The walls absorb and release heat. Runoff is recovered from the lawns and brought to the garden. Jean-Marie and Charlotte are waiting for us in the sonar cylinder. It's art by Bernhard Leitner, something about integrating the concepts of space and sound in a natural setting."

"You've done your research," Nico said.

Two narrow paths led to the concrete cylinder. Despite the acclaimed artist's goal of creating a life-affirming space within the bamboo garden, it had served as a perfect predator's trap on this night. The victim was still swimming in his own blood.

"Have you started examining the body?" Nico asked.

Three factors had to be considered: the location, the victim's clothes, and the condition of the corpse.

"Yes," said Commander Maurin. She was one of the most organized members of Nico's team. "The victim died from a knife wound to his torso. We haven't found the weapon. His name was Mathieu Leroy. He was twenty-three years old. He was studying to be a math teacher. He had a student ID his wallet. And a condom."

Nico crouched by the body. Mathieu was rather handsome and well-dressed. Nico guessed he had planned to go out and have a good time. But he had come across a monster—maybe more than one. Had a chance encounter gone wrong? Or was it an evening with friends that turned sour? The result was the same either way: he'd been stabbed to death. But there was something else.

"His shoulder's a mess," Deputy Chief Jean-Marie Rost said.

"It's actually been cut up," Claire Le Marec added. "Some of it's completely missing."

His jacket and shirt had been torn away from the neck, and a chunk of muscle and skin had been cut out.

"He pissed his pants," Rost said. "Scared stiff, apparently."

"Any clues?"

"Hair," Le Marec said. "Mathieu probably pulled his aggressor's hair, so it should be in at least one of his hands."

Mathieu had struggled, but the murderer hadn't given him much of a chance. A single thrust into the abdomen. The wound was still fresh. There hadn't been any hesitation.

"Why would he take a piece of the shoulder?" Le Marec asked.

"Cannibalism?" Rost offered. "Maybe a snack for breakfast."

"You're too much," Maurin said.

Her colleague gave her a dark smile.

"Why not?" Nico said. "There's no limit to depravity. Have you been in touch with the medical examiner's office?"

"We have," Maurin replied.

Nico stood up and scanned the interior of the cylinder.

"The water usually flows down the walls, and there's electronic music," Maurin explained. "The park officials turned them off when they found the body."

Nico nodded.

"The park's going to be the talk of the town," he said. "A buried skeleton and now this murder. We'll have to get the area cordoned off. Kriven can help. We'll make the arrangements in the morning."

Nico looked back at Mathieu Leroy. Why had Mathieu been in this isolated place in the middle of the night? Had he come with someone? Maurin's group would have to go through the victim's life, interview his family and friends, and put together a timeline of the hours leading up to his visit to the park.

Telling his family would be the worst part.

11

Holding two coffees, David Kriven made his way up the stairs and through the obstacle course of the top-floor halls. The floor creaked underfoot. Kriven felt like he was walking through an old, decaying hotel. He glanced at his mugs to make sure the steaming liquid hadn't spilled.

Finally, he reached the criminal psychologist's office. The door was half open. Before he could open it all the way, he spotted a spider hanging by its thread from the ceiling. A spider in the morning: a sure sign of impending sorrow, his grandmother had once told him. She had died at a fairly young age. Apparently the janitors weren't superstitious, because they hadn't cleaned this particular corner.

"Dominique?" he asked. "It's David."

"Come in!"

He opened the door with his foot and set the mugs on the desk. The room was so small, squeezing in more than two people would have been quite a feat. A narrow window with bars added to the cell-like feel. Not the most pleasant place to work. Only the poster for *Men in Black II* lent any cheer to the room.

"You should update your poster," Kriven said.

Dominique Kreiss smiled. She was a curvaceous brunette with green eyes that twinkled roguishly. These days she was in a much better mood than she was a year ago, when she was living with a creep. She had finally gotten rid of him. Evidently, even shrinks made mistakes.

"Thanks for the coffee," she said as she grabbed a tissue to wipe a few drops off her desk. "Got any news?"

"Anya Sirsky's alive," David said as he sat down. "That's all I know, really."

"That's good. So what brings you here?"

"You mean, aside from *you*?" he asked. It was no secret that he was attracted to this psychologist.

"I met Mrs. Cassian," he said. "Her son vanished thirty years ago, but his room is in exactly the same state as it was when he left. And she talks about him as though he were still alive."

"For some people, it's more complicated to accept a loved one's disappearance than his death. Questions remain unanswered, and the hope that the loved one is still alive strips away regular points of reference. Believing that he's dead would be a betrayal. It's a terrible place to be in. What you're telling me makes perfect sense."

"That's not all. Almeida found wrapped presents crammed in the closet. It just seems crazy."

"The loss of a child—whether it's a death or a disappearance—is a blow. A parent with a fragile psychological makeup could develop a defense system just to cope and hold onto the belief that the child is still alive. It's not uncommon for a parent to keep cooking meals for the child, setting a place at the table, or washing his clothes. Perhaps in this case, the mother kept buying birthday and Christmas gifts for her son."

"That's morbid."

Dominique Kreiss held her tongue. She knew that Commander Kriven and his wife had lost their newborn child some time back and it had taken a toll on their relationship.

"It's a traumatic experience," she said after a pause. "Fortunately, most people who suffer this kind of tragedy survive and deal with the loss. Although they're never the same again, they can go on and lead full lives."

"How should we behave around Mrs. Cassian?"

"It's not a good idea to appeal to logic with her or to force her to face the reality that her son is gone. I recommend going along with her belief system."

"That's exactly how we were able to obtain our evidence, but I'm concerned about the ethics."

"You did the right thing."

"Chief Sirsky and I have to interview Samuel Cassian today. He doesn't know that the bones we found in the pit are actually his son's or that his son was buried there after his disappearance."

"I'd advise you talk to him and his wife separately. And don't forget that Samuel Cassian has returned to the site of the banquet several times. He's going to realize all at once that he's been walking over his son's grave. He's in for a nasty shock."

Kriven got up, unnerved by the thought.

"How about we grab a bite to eat tonight?" he asked offhandedly.

"No, I've got work to finish for the juvenile delinquency division. Michel Cohen wants my report on his desk before midnight."

"I'll order a pizza. We'll make it quick, I promise. You can't wait till midnight to eat."

Nico set down the preliminary report. Deputy Chief Jean-Marie Rost had summarized the events and carefully described each step of the investigation. The only parts left were Samuel Cassian's interview and the DNA identification, which would come the next morning. The DNA analysis was just a formality. They had enough evidence, including Professor Vilars's dental identification. After thirty years of uncertainty, Jean-Baptiste Cassian's disappearance was no longer a mystery. He had been murdered and buried in a location that was deeply significant for his family—and probably for the criminal too, even though they still didn't know the murderer's motives.

Captain Plassard's interviews hadn't uncovered any leads. Witnesses at the banquet-performance, the dig, and the discovery of the bones had nothing of note to add, although they all expressed respect for Samuel Cassian's work, appreciation for his friendship, sadness over the disappearance of his son, and admiration for the young man.

Within forty-eight hours, Christine Lormes, the public prosecutor, would have everything she needed to close the preliminary investigation, open a criminal investigation, and name an investigating magistrate. Questions about the statute of limitations and the nature of their intervention would inevitably arise; these points of law would have to be resolved as quickly as possible. In any case, they would have to make a miracle happen; the crime was three decades old.

Nico looked at the pictures Lieutenant Almeida had found in Jean-Baptiste Cassian's room. In most of them, Jean-Baptiste was with friends. One, in particular, caught his eye. In it, he had his arm around a young woman. Was she his girlfriend? Nico went through the rest of the pictures. Then he held up a few of the victim alone. These weren't ordinary photos, like the others. They were portraits of Jean-Baptiste. They looked like they had been taken by someone who wasn't just a casual friend. This photographer seemed to be more than that. Who was this person?

Nico got up from his chair and stretched. He had gotten only a few hours of sleep. Maurin's group had started the investigation immediately, and the body found in the Leitner Cylinder would be autopsied that day. They would soon know more. That wasn't foremost in his mind, though. He was thinking of his mother lying in that hospital bed, hooked to machines. He wanted to tell himself that everything would be okay, but he was scared stiff. Like Dimitri, who had insisted on going to school even though he had spent most of the night worrying, Nico knew he had to stay focused.

At the end of the fourth-floor hallway, Nico knocked on an ordinary-looking door that led directly to the prosecutors' offices and was one of the building's best-kept secrets. He greeted the secretaries, walked into another hallway, and knocked on the door of Christine Lormes's office. She was now officially in charge of what they were now calling the Skeletor case.

"Please come in. Have a seat," Lormes said. "I heard about your mother. This can't be the easiest time for you. But we have to keep going, don't we?"

"Thank you. The next few days will be critical. Fingers crossed."

Lormes gave him a sympathetic smile. "Where are you with the preliminary report on the Cassian case?"

"It should be in your hands tomorrow morning. I'm still waiting for the DNA analysis. Our suspicions of murder have been confirmed. As you know, the victim, Jean-Baptiste Cassian, disappeared thirty years ago. An investigation into his disappearance was opened three weeks after the burial of the *tableau-piège* in the Parc de la Villette. His parents had reported him missing. We've combed that file for every detail."

"You're probably already aware, Chief Sirsky, that we have a problem. The statute of limitations for criminal cases begins on the day a crime is committed, according to article seven of the Criminal Procedure Code. In the past, whenever we've tried to date the statute of limitations from the day a homicide is discovered, arguing that ignorance of the crime *de facto* called for the suspension of said period, the court of appeals has never agreed. So even though murderers usually do everything they can to conceal their crime, the ten-year limit has been repeatedly upheld. That said, I've been knee-deep in legal research to find a work-around."

"But there was the missing-persons investigation," Nico said. "We might have that going for us."

"No, apparently not. The time limit is ten years, and it can be suspended only if there's an intervening investigation or prosecution during that time period. If there was, as is the case here, the clock starts ticking with the last official act. It appears that we're roughly twenty years past the time limit."

"You've been looking for a loophole?" Nico asked hopefully.

"Professor Vilars said the death occurred twenty-five to thirty-five years ago. At this point, we have no definitive proof that the death and the disappearance happened at the same time. In addition, there's still some uncertainty as to the actual cause of death."

The prosecutor paused. Professor Vilars's conclusions gave them some leeway. She was a precise and sharp medical examiner, and Nico suspected that she had deliberately made her conclusions somewhat ambiguous. He would have to thank her the next time he saw her.

"I believe the appeals court wouldn't be opposed to opening an investigation into the date and cause of death. However, any indictment for murder, if you find the culprit, is uncertain, at best."

"Many things could happen in the meantime," Nico said. "I also wanted to talk to you about the archaeological dig."

"Yes?"

"Only a quarter of the site has been exhumed. We need to check the entire site."

"I was hoping we could avoid that," Lormes replied. "The bigwigs are pressuring us about the press coverage. The Ministry of Culture has a lot hanging on this."

"It's crucial to our investigation."

"I understand, but what guarantees can you provide that this won't turn into *CSI La Villette*? We'd have the entire culture and art set making a big fuss, and we all know how creative they can get about fusses."

"The Society for the Disinterment of the *Tableau-Piège* could modify its plans and organize a complete dig under the eyes of the forensics investigators, couldn't they?"

"That would be a good compromise," Lormes said. With his son's murder, I doubt Cassian will be that invested in what becomes of his final banquet. It's all very complicated. I'll keep you updated. Please do the same for me."

"I'll be meeting with Cassian later this morning."

"Good. Now let's talk about the Mathieu Leroy murder. At this rate, I'll have to put together a crisis team for the Parc de la Villette."

"I'm afraid there isn't much to say. My team has been working on it, and they know it's a priority."

"Fine. As with the Cassian case, keep me in the loop," the prosecutor said.

Back in his office, Nico called Caroline. She picked up immediately.

"Any news?" he asked.

"I talked to Dr. Fursac. They took her off the sedatives this morning. Anya's been moving a bit."

"What does that mean?"

"It's a good sign. It means she's waking up. But let's not jump to conclusions yet. We still have to wait. I'll call you early this afternoon."

"Thank you, my love."

He could almost hear her smiling.

He ended the call and went to find Kriven in the Coquibus room. Together, they left the building. They took Nico's car, driving along the Seine toward Saint-Germain-des-Prés and Cassian's apartment. The artist had returned home after two nights in the hospital. He was probably exhausted, but the meeting couldn't be delayed any longer.

Mrs. Cassian opened the door. They followed her into the sitting room, where her husband was stretched out on the couch with two pillows and a comforter. His face was pale, and there were purplish rings under his eye. Distress was sucking the energy right out of him.

Samuel Cassian pushed away the cover and got up slowly.

"Good day, sirs," he said in a raspy voice. Nico made out a slight accent. Cassian's heritage was Romanian, and despite his international stature, he clung to his roots. Cassian held out a hand and Nico shook it with a firm grip, not wanting to treat him like a sick old man.

"I'm Chief Sirsky, in charge of Paris's Criminal Investigation Division, and this is Commander Kriven."

"You're from 36 Quai des Orfévres? One of those Simenon cops?"

"Yes, just like Inspector Maigret," Nico said.

Cassian's eyes twinkled. They'd connected.

Nico smiled and then realized that Mrs. Cassian was in the room too. She hadn't said a word. She was staring at Kriven, who was holding her son's dental X-rays. Seeing the agony of loss in her eyes, Nico felt a pit in his stomach. For half a second he saw his mother lying in that hospital bed, hooked to an IV and monitoring lines. He turned back to Mr. Cassian.

"Dear, could you get us something to drink?" her husband asked, lowering himself back onto the couch and gesturing to the officers to sit down.

The woman wrung her hands, looked at the X-rays again, and went off to the kitchen.

"So you have things to tell me and questions to ask," Samuel Cassian said.

"We have information about the skeleton that was found at the archaeological dig," Nico said carefully.

"It's fine, Inspector. We both know where you're headed."

His look of absolute despair contradicted his seeming sangfroid.

"It belonged to a young adult who died thirty years ago, about five and a half feet tall, with a broken tibia."

Samuel Cassian nodded, his eyes full of tears.

"How did he die?" His voice was becoming even raspier.

"A blow to the head. He died instantly and didn't suffer."

There was silence. Cassian slumped, engulfed in grief. Nico couldn't take his eyes off him. The man's troubled breathing sounded like the machines keeping Anya alive. Nico had that sinking feeling again, the man's pain resonating with his own uncertainty about his mother's future.

Samuel Cassian looked up. "You're going to find who took my son, aren't you?"

"We're working on it," Nico said in his most professional tone. Then he went quiet again. He looked Cassian in the eye and said, "I'll find the person who did this. I promise."

Nico heard Kriven clear his throat. He had gone too far. They never made promises to victims' families. What was he doing? But this man, this death, and the timing were affecting him in a way that he had never been affected before. He had to give the Cassians some peace of mind. He had to do this for them. And for his mother.

Cassian was the one to break the silence. "Are you absolutely sure it's our son?"

"The dental records match. We're still waiting for a DNA analysis," Kriven said, setting the X-rays on the coffee table.

"Mr. Cassian, you said you had lunch with your son the day he disappeared. Do you know what kind of watch he was wearing?"

"A Rolex Explorer II. I'd given it to him not long before the banquet. It was a sort of early thank you for all the work he had put in."

"Do you remember what he was wearing?"

"Very clearly. Jeans and Adidas. He loved those shoes. They were all the rage."

Samuel Cassian had had time to think through all these details—three decades. Thirty-one years. They were the same details recorded in the police report that they had retrieved from the archives.

"These items were found in the pit, close to the skeleton," Nico said to quash any false hopes.

"So what do you want to know?" Cassian asked.

"Did your son have any enemies?"

"He was twenty-two years old! He grew up in a free country at a time when kids like him didn't have a worry in the world. How could he have had any enemies? I lived through the war in Romania, and believe me, Jean-Baptiste's life was a far cry from that."

"Was anybody jealous of him? There had to be someone. People must have thought his success in the art world wasn't earned, that you helped him get a foot in the door."

"They'd be idiots. Jean-Baptiste had real talent. He would have been better than me if he'd lived."

Parents always hoped their children would be better than they were, especially if they followed in their footsteps. Nico knew this all too well. Dimitri had told him on Christmas Eve that he wanted to go to the police academy. Nico would worry every day his son was on the job, but he was proud of the boy.

"You know that it takes more than talent," Nico said.

"But talent is key. If my son hadn't had the skill and passion for painting, I wouldn't have been able to help him."

"Is there any chance you were the target? Could someone have been angry with you and taken vengeance in this way?"

Samuel Cassian took a deep breath. "I don't see how. I've always thought it was important to support others in the arts and bring people together."

Nico spread the photos from Jean-Baptiste's bedroom on the table. Their host looked at them carefully. Nico could see the wistfulness on his face.

"He was so happy to be alive. He smiled all the time. A good boy, really. The son I'd always dreamed of."

As Dimitri was for him, Nico thought. And he owed Sylvie on that score. Sylvie was the reason he had a son. And for that gift alone, she would always be able to count on him.

"That's Lara," Cassian said. "His fiancée. She was so charming. They met in art school."

Nico looked at Kriven, who took the signal and asked, "What's happened to her?"

The man shrugged. "At first, we stayed in touch. Then we gradually stopped seeing each other and writing. I pushed her away. She needed to move on with her life."

"Lara what?"

"Lara Krall, like Diana Krall, the jazz singer."

"Did they really love each other?"

"I'd say they did, but not in a showy way."

"And they didn't fight?"

"Not as far as I knew."

"Did you know where her family lived?"

"Her parents had property in Tours. Her father owned a business, and her mother was a teacher."

Mrs. Cassian came back in and set a tray on the table with tea, fruit juice, liqueurs, and a bottle of premier-cru Montagny wine. She turned around quickly and left the room.

"Was Lara a photographer?" Nico asked.

"Hmm, not that I remember."

"Who took these?" Kriven asked, pointing to the pictures of Jean-Baptiste.

"No idea. Our son was twenty-two. He had a life of his own."

"But he lived with you," Kriven said.

"He spent some time at Lara's place and some at ours. She had a studio apartment in the Latin Quarter."

"And the group pictures?" Nico asked.

Phase three of questioning was now under way. They were pressing the witness to draw out more information or bring additional memories to the fore.

"A friend, probably."

"But who?"

"I have no idea!"

His Romanian accent was becoming more pronounced as the tension rose.

Mrs. Cassian came back with a plate of *petits-fours*.

"Dear, can you bring me the invitation to Jean-Baptiste's exhibition in New York? I want to show it to our guests." It seemed that Samuel Cassian was used to telling his wife what to do.

"Oh yes! You should have seen it. His canvases were wonderful. That's what the critics said. Such a young boy and already a great artist," she said as she left the room once again.

"Could you give us his friends' names?" Kriven said. "You must remember at least a few of them, especially now that you're seeing their faces."

"Give me your notebook," the artist said to Kriven. "These young men in particular and my son were inseparable. I'll write down their names while you open that bottle of Burgundy. It's an excellent vintage from the Chalon coast."

Kriven poured three glasses as their host moved the pen over the paper.

"Have a taste, Chief."

Nico brought the glass to his lips, breathed in the aromas, and took a sip. It was fresh and fruity. Cassian handed him the notebook and picked up his own glass.

"Excellent," Cassian said, with a refined smack of the lips. "Life has its little pleasures. They don't chase away our troubles, but they help us keep going. I presume you'll take up a fresh investigation of Jean-Baptiste's disappearance. When we reported him missing, your colleagues came up blank, although I'm sure they put in a good-faith effort. I kept hounding them but finally gave up, realizing it wouldn't change anything."

Yes, Nico thought, they had given up, and at that moment, the clock on the statute of limitations had started ticking, making it highly unlikely that they could prosecute the murderer, even if they found out who did it.

"There's something else," Nico said quietly. "We'll be questioning everyone who was at the banquet and examining more of the site. We don't want to miss something crucial to the investigation."

Samuel Cassian froze.

"We can solve this mystery while seeing to it that your work progresses in a systematic and controlled way. The Society for the Disinterment of the *Tableau-Piège* and the police will work hand in hand. What do you think?" Nico was asking out of respect for the artist. The man's approval or disapproval would not change the investigation.

"I don't know what to say."

"You don't need to be involved. It's your choice. But the organization probably will reach out to you."

Mrs. Cassian came in again, excited and happy, waving the invitation to the opening of their son's exhibition, *New York, New York.*

"'Start spreading the news.'" Cassian's voice cracked when he got to the next line. "'I'm leaving today.'"

On their way back to headquarters, Kriven was quieter than usual. He was shifting in his seat.

"What is it, David? Spit it out."

"Um, well, it must be hard for you, boss, with your mom and all. You know you can count on me if you need some time off with your family."

Nico looked over at Kriven. "We have a job to do, and I have a promise to keep."

"About that," Kriven said. "You see, you made a promise to Cassian, Chief, and, um, we never do that."

Nico kept his eyes on the road. He didn't have a response.

"I'm just worried, boss, that it's becoming personal for you."

There was a long moment of silence. Nico pulled into his parking spot and turned to Kriven. "David, fighting crime is always personal."

12

The apartment where Nico's mother lived was decorated tastefully in a contemporary style. But it also highlighted her heritage. *Psankas*, the renowned Ukrainian Easter eggs, gleamed in an elegant showcase. What irony, Nico thought, as he picked one up: a pagan symbol that had become a central part of the Christian rite of Easter, a springtime celebration invented by worshippers of the sun god, Dazhboh. They believed that birds were Dazhboh's chosen species, because they could get close to him. Eggs, a magical source of life, had become a symbol for the resurrection of Christ.

Anya had turned Nico's bedroom into a library, where she spent her winter evenings reading and rereading her favorite authors. That way, she said, she would always feel her son's presence, as when she had told him the stories of Kiev and Russia and recited lines from novels and poems to help him sleep. She still kept a copy of the *Stories of Times Past*, a book of legends, in this room. "Here are the stories of times past, from the land of Russia, whose kings first ruled in Kiev, where the Russian lands started." And Nico would never forget. Vladimir, grand prince of Kiev, was converted to Byzantine-Rite Christianity in 988, subordinating the entire Russian Church to the patriarchate in Constantinople, bringing orthodoxy forevermore to the Slavic lands, and banishing the old pagan beliefs to darkness. It was the history of his ancestors engraved in his soul.

In the kitchen, Nico found the oversized *matryoshka* nesting doll inherited from his great-grandmother. Everything was in its place. An entire tsar-cut smoked salmon and a container of caviar, both from Petrossian, were on the top shelf of the refrigerator. Anya liked to nibble salmon and caviar while sipping vodka from a champagne flute. He tried to imagine her back in this apartment soon, with her books and caviar.

Nico walked out on the balcony on the building's sixth floor. Before him lay the grandest view of the capital, or so his mother claimed: the Alexandre Nevsky Cathedral on the Rue Daru. Each of its five spires was topped with a gilded onion dome and the Russian Orthodox cross with three horizontal crossbeams. The pediment's face bore a Murano-mosaic representation of Christ, a halo around his head. The Savior was sitting on a throne, blessing the world with his right hand and holding the Gospel open on his left knee. Nico recited his mother's favorite verse. "I am the light of the world: he that followeth me shall not walk in darkness, but shall have the light of life. I am the door: by me if any man enter in, he shall be saved, and shall go in and out, and find pasture." As his voice rose, he felt close to tears. That was his entire childhood right there.

Back inside, he ran his fingers over the blooms on the snowball tree. The white flowers were already bursting in large umbels. The tree was a national symbol of Ukraine, symbolizing both love and marriage. It had inspired the famous song "Kalinka." Anya hummed it whenever the family gathered for dinner. Even Dimitri knew the naughty words by heart.

Memories and images were flooding back. Nico closed his eyes for a few seconds and saw his son sitting on his tricycle, watching as colorful balloons, which had escaped his grasp, began floating away. He saw Dimitri urging him to catch them before they rose any higher. He heard Dimitri laugh, and when he looked back, he saw Anya, who had been with them that day, with tears running down her cheeks. She had been crying and laughing at the same time. That scene had occurred just a few weeks after his father had died, and she had still been grieving for him.

Anya, with her warmth, good cheer, and generosity, had always been the matriarch in the best sense of the word. His father had called her something else, a *tarpan*: the storied wild horse that roamed the Ukrainian steppes by the Black Sea. It was said that a similar horse roamed Poland's forests. And so these two indomitable personalities—Anya and his father—seemed fated to join forces. The story always made Nico and his sister smile.

Nico's thoughts turned to Tanya; they'd both been in a fug since the day before. Their text messages were their link to one another as they waited until six o'clock, when they could be back at Anya's bedside. They wanted to be there when she woke up. Nico was furious that he couldn't do anything more than wait.

Nico ruminated as he watched the play of light on the cathedral's domes. Anya had her faith. Maybe she was right. He looked at the cross and called out, "I'll find Cassian's murderer. You save Anya."

His phone vibrated. He hoped it was Caroline.

It was Commander Maurin.

"I've just left the medical examiner's office," she said. "We've got a cause of death for Mathieu Leroy: the penetrating wound resulted in a hemopneumothorax. Both air and blood rushed into the pleural cavity. The pain would have been unbearable. Cardiac and respiratory failure was inevitable. The wound was inflicted by a knife. It was a characteristic stab wound with clean edges. Given the appearance of the wound, the blade probably had only one sharp edge."

"An ordinary knife," Nico said, irritated that there wasn't more to distinguish it.

"Okay, that won't help us find the murderer. The victim didn't have any cuts on his hands or arms; all evidence suggests that he didn't try to defend himself."

"The aggressor was dominating his prey."

"A man? The knife was thrust in the torso with quite a bit of force."

"The crime itself would suggest as much. What did Professor Vilars make of the shoulder?"

"The criminal hacked away the trapezius muscle after death and took a piece about two and a half inches square. It wasn't a pretty sight. And it wasn't a professional who did the cutting. It was done in a haphazard way. We can't even tell if he was left-handed or right."

"Did Professor Vilars notice anything unusual about the body?"

"Nothing at all."

"And anything from the forensics lab?"

"Not just yet. The hairs we found at the crime scene are synthetic. They came from a wig."

Nico frowned. "A disguise," he said. "What do we know about Mathieu Leroy?"

"Not much about his past. His friends at school liked him. He was a bachelor. We'll keep looking."

"He was found in the middle of the night in the Parc de la Villette, the victim of someone—probably a man—who was wearing a hairpiece. We've got plenty to do. Keep looking."

Nico and Tanya stopped at the nurses' desk before going into his mother's room.

"How's she doing?" Nico asked.

The nurse looked at her computer screen and read off her vitals.

"Her heart rate is still high, and her blood pressure's low. We'll have to get her stabilized a bit more before we can take her off the ventilator."

Nico thanked the nurse and slipped his hand into Tanya's. She was really more than a sister. She was as good as his twin. She had been with him through thick and thin. And she was with him now, in this small corner of Bichat Hospital, where Death eagerly watched its prey.

13

The morning was sunny and surprisingly warm for early spring. Gaetan Roussel's lyrics flowed through Nico's car. Roussel's "Inside Outside," a catchy acoustic-pop tune with a contemporary refrain, seemed to suit his mood.

In front of headquarters, two security officers in bulletproof vests stood guard as the red-and-white gate rose. Nico pulled into his parking spot. He walked through the interior courtyard and up Stairwell A to the fourth floor. He nodded to his secretary, Rachel.

"Professor Queneau wants to talk to you, Chief," she said.

"Put a call through to him right away."

"And your mother?"

"She was able to squeeze my hand last night. She's doing better."

He walked down the narrow corridor to his office. His phone was ringing before he even sat down.

"Professor Queneau? Chief Sirsky here."

"It's good to hear your voice. How is your mother?"

"I think we're past the worst part. That's my hope."

"Good, Nico. I have the DNA analyses here. The skeleton is Jean-Baptiste Cassian's."

"Now we can close the preliminary report. While I have you on the phone, I suspect you'll be asked to supervise the rest of the excavation."

"You mean the rest of the *tableau-piège* is going to be dug up?"

"I don't see how else this investigation can play out. I think Samuel Cassian is willing to work with us."

"Okay, I'll come up with a plan. Thanks for the heads-up."

Michel Cohen came in without knocking. His cigar preceded him, and the white smoke, along with its unpleasant odor, filled the room. As usual, Nico refrained from saying anything. His superior's authority, established by a legendary career, absolved him.

"I'll be in touch with you later, Professor," Nico said as he hung up.

Cohen was a short man whose dense features seemed to compensate for his lack of stature. He had bushy black hair and thick brows above penetrating eyes. His nose was large. Cohen was a man who made his presence known. He walked over to Nico's desk and tossed a pile of newspapers on it.

"Check out the morning's headlines," he said.

"Security at the Parc de la Villette: fact or folly?" one of the tabloid headlines read. "Weeping in the City of Blood," declared another headline. "The Butcher of Paris rises again," read a third.

"The reporters are going to town with this," Cohen said. "You know what I always say in these cases."

Nico did know. "When the shit hits the fan, everyone gets splashed."

"Wrap this Leroy thing up quickly."

"That's the plan."

"As for the Cassian banquet, it looks like a long list of VIP guests and potential suspects. The chance one of them will cry foul is huge. So be careful going through everything. You know the deal: too many people at a party, not enough Champagne to go around, and then everyone's on edge," Cohen said. "Oh, and Nicole asked me if you needed to take a few days off."

Police Commissioner Nicole Monthalet was looking out for him. Some people thought she was a bit cold, but it was hard to find a better cop and leader.

"She also said you could do the impossible, which right now means dealing with two murders, the excavation in the Parc de la Villette, and a mother in the hospital."

"The impossible? That's my middle name," Nico said.

Cohen, his spiritual father and his protector, stared at him for a second. Then he winked—his typical gesture of encouragement.

"Perfect. Keep me updated."

Nico nodded. Jean-Baptiste Cassian's murderer *and* the Butcher of Paris for Anya's life. Amen.

Commander Kriven handed Deputy Chief Jean-Marie Rost a coffee, and they walked down the hall to Nico's office, greeting Michel Cohen, who was heading in the other direction. They were quieter than usual. Kriven wasn't in the mood for bantering.

"Chief," he said to Nico as they entered the office. The boss looked both of them over.

"Your hair's all messed up," he told Kriven with a smile.

"Didn't sleep well," Kriven said.

"Oh, really? I saw you taking pizza into Dominique's office last night," Rost said.

"We just talked."

His late-night pizza dinner with Dominique Kreiss had lasted until four in the morning. It was more than conversation. Kreiss, the shrink, had hit him with some hard truths. Losing a child could tear a couple apart. He and his wife had failed to conceive another child after losing their first, and Kriven had quit trying. But Kreiss brought him around to his real feelings: he still loved Clara.

"You were up talking all night?" Rost asked.

"Yep," Kriven said, focusing on Nico. "Lara Krall Weissman just came in. How should we deal with her?"

"I'm still catching up," Nico said. "Take her up to the interview room. Jean-Marie? You can finish the preliminary report. Professor Queneau sent over the DNA results. It's a match."

"I'll have it on your desk by the time the interview's over."

"Is Plassard still dealing with the VIPs involved with the *tableau-piège*?"

"Slaving away at it," Kriven said.

The photos they had picked up at the Cassian apartment were spread on Nico's desk.

"Have you looked over the names of Jean-Baptiste's friends that Samuel Cassian added to your notebook?" Nico asked Kriven.

"I'm on it. I'll have an update for you by the end of the morning."

Nico held up a photo of Jean-Baptiste Cassian and Lara Krall, surrounded by their happy friends.

"That hammer might have been swung by a woman," he said.

Climbing the stairs to the interview room, Nico skimmed over Kriven's notes on Lara Krall. She lived on the Rue Dumont d'Urville in the sixteenth arrondissement, in a corner apartment by the Place des États-Unis. It probably had a view of the Square Thomas-Jefferson. She was married to Gregory Weissman and had taken his last name. He owned one of the largest recruiting firms in Paris, with branches in Lyon, Bordeaux, and Marseilles. She was a stay-at-home mother of two teenagers. She had come a long way since the École des Beaux-Arts.

The officer on duty ushered Nico in. He took care to look relaxed, as he didn't want to unnerve the middle-aged woman who was a smiling girl in the photos he had just looked at.

"Mrs. Weissman, have you been followed the news? Have you read about the excavation of Samuel Cassian's *tableau-piège* in the Parc de la Villette?"

"Yes, I've seen the stories," she said, sounding wary.

"And you were engaged to his son, Jean-Baptiste?"

"Thirty years ago, yes."

"Did you meet at the École des Beaux-Arts?"

"Yes, he was absolutely charming. I admired his talent."

"What were you studying? Photography?"

"Sculpture," she said, looking at her hands.

Nico sensed resignation.

"I stopped doing all that a long time ago," she said. "I'm too busy with my family. There's just no time."

She was lying. Managing the lives of her husband and children couldn't fill the void in her heart. Why had she stopped sculpting? Because Jean-Baptiste had disappeared? Or because she couldn't stand doing it after she killed him and buried him in his father's most acclaimed creation?

"And you've never wanted to go back to it?"

"It's not my husband's cup of tea, and that suits me."

"So you lost both your fiancé and your art. Two parts of yourself. Is there anything left of your twenties?"

"What business is that of yours?" she asked abruptly.

"When he disappeared, Jean-Baptiste was surprisingly successful," Nico said, ignoring her anger. "Both in Paris and in New York. It makes me wonder. People had to be jealous of his success. Without his father, he probably wouldn't have catapulted to fame quite as easily."

"There's always backstabbing. But I was too young to pay any attention, and Jean-Baptiste had real talent. Nobody denied that. The art critics in New York praised him to heaven."

"And you? Nothing in New York or Paris?"

"I had plenty of time ahead of me. That was what I felt."

"But not now?"

"I just told you that I'm busy with other things."

"Did Jean-Baptiste get along with his father?"

"With Samuel?" Lara Krall asked, puzzled. "He loved him! He wanted to follow in his father's footsteps. His dream was to have a career as rich and brilliant as Samuel's. He just wanted his father to be proud of him."

Nico set the pictures on the table. Lara winced.

"Who took these pictures of the group?"

"Daniel Vion. He's not in any of the pictures, though. He didn't like being in front of the camera."

"Who are the friends around you?"

"These two are Jérôme Dufour and Michel Géko. To their right are Nathan Sellière and Sophie Bayle. Laurent Mercier and Camille Frot were seeing each other."

Nico pulled out the portraits of Jean-Baptiste Cassian. Lara's eyes grew wide. She started breathing quickly.

"What's wrong?" Nico asked.

"Well… It's just that… I haven't seen him since… I put all that behind me, you know."

"I understand. Were these taken by Daniel?"

"I don't know. I've never seen these pictures."

"They're awfully *intimate*, don't you think? I even thought you might have been the one who took them," Nico said pointedly.

She sat up in her chair.

"Do you remember the day Jean-Baptiste disappeared?"

"We were planning to have dinner together at my studio, and he was going to spend the night. I waited, but he never came."

"You must have been worried."

She shrugged.

"Had he let you down like that before?" Nico asked. "Did you have reason to believe something was keeping him elsewhere?"

She pursed her lips.

"He was seeing someone else, wasn't he?"

Lara sighed and looked down.

"How did you figure it out?" Nico asked.

"He didn't seem to be attracted to me the way he was when we met. He wasn't as excited when we made love. And it was less and less often."

"That's all?"

"There was one week when he seemed unusually secretive. He was nervous about my seeing him without his shirt on. Then I accidently went into the bathroom when he was there, and I found out why. He had a bite mark on his shoulder!"

Nico shuddered. A bite on the shoulder. An implicitly sexual act.

"I was livid. I wanted to know who the woman was."

"Which of your friends was he sleeping with? Sophie or Camille? Someone else?"

"Neither of them! He swore that he could never touch another woman, that I was the only one, and that he loved me. He wanted to marry me. That wasn't it."

"Then what was it?"

"He said he had tried something else to experience different feelings."

"What was this different experience?"

"A man." Lara sighed again.

"A man?"

"Yes. I thought it was my fault. I wasn't enough for him."

"Who was this man?"

"Jean-Baptiste didn't want to tell me. He swore that it was just a one-night stand. He could never have the same kind of love with this person that he had with me."

"And that explanation was enough for you?"

"I was twenty-two years old. I loved him. I wasn't ready to give up," she said. Her voice was thick with emotion.

"I read the police report on his disappearance. There was nothing about this."

"It was private."

"Did his parents know?"

"I was the only one. There was no reason Jean-Baptiste would have told them. It didn't mean anything."

"But he disappeared," Nico said. "Mrs. Weissman, I'm sorry to tell you this. Jean-Baptiste is dead."

She was silent. "The skeleton," she finally said.

"Jean-Baptiste was murdered and buried in the *tableau-piège*. We think it's possible that an argument got out of control."

"Are you implying that I might have had something to do with this? I loved him. We were engaged!"

"But he had an affair, and it was with a man. That would raise questions in any other homicide investigation, don't you think?"

"But I had decided to keep his secret. I was ready to forget about it and move on."

"Still, it was a betrayal."

"An artist has to have new experiences."

Nico decided not to press the matter.

"How did he die?" she asked.

"He was hit on the head with a hammer."

"My God! Who would do such a thing?"

"One of your friends, out of jealousy?"

"But we were all very close. We were so happy for Jean-Baptiste's success."

"When did you meet Gregory Weissman?"

"Five years after Jean-Baptiste's disappearance. He didn't know Jean-Baptiste or any of our friends."

"Very well. I don't have any other questions right now. But I must ask you not to leave Paris until this crime has been solved. We'll probably need to bring you in again."

Lara Weissman seemed lost, bereft. Either she was a very good actress, or her life had just taken another unexpected turn. Jean-Baptiste hadn't just disappeared, hadn't just left her behind, but had been murdered. He was dead.

Fifteen minutes later, the chief of the Criminal Investigation Division took the preliminary report, which had been sitting on his desk, over to the prosecutor.

Lormes flipped through it.

"Opening an investigation to find the date and exact cause of death seems appropriate. We can't investigate a specific person for murder, due to the statute of limitations, but lifting the veil on this affair is certainly in order. Jean-Baptiste Cassian's disappearance has been a mystery all these years and has caused his parents to suffer. I hope we'll be able to tell them exactly when and how he died. And perhaps the investigation will shed some light on the murderer."

"I agree."

"Only three days have gone by since the skeleton was discovered, and you've determined the probable cause of death and the victim's identity. Well done, Chief. At this point, some of my colleagues would consider the investigation more or less resolved. No point in finding the murderer or determining the motives. I don't share that opinion. I believe you'll be able to get to the bottom of this, and I have faith in the magistrate who'll make the final decision."

Nico left the prosecutor's office and headed toward Claire Le Marec's.

"Where are you with Maurin?"

"We were putting the finishing touches on the victim's profile and trying to unearth the trail."

"What do you have?" Claire Le Marec asked.

A deal, Nico said to himself. His mother's life in exchange for a promise to find Jean-Baptiste Cassian murderer. And that person could possibly be the one who murdered the young man in the Leitner Cylinder. But he couldn't tell Le Marec about that.

"Jean-Baptiste Cassian had cheated on his fiancée with a man before he disappeared. According to Lara Krall, it was a one-time experience, something that he did to expand himself artistically. Nobody else knew."

The eighties, the glitzy decade that saw the rise of MTV, consumerism, and a new generation of dance clubs, had also seen the stirrings of public acceptance of gay and lesbian love. Soft Cell's "Tainted Love" and Frankie Goes to Hollywood's "Relax" were both hits. In 1981, a huge gay-pride parade had taken place in the streets of Paris to press François Mitterrand to lower the age of consent for gays and lesbians. And in 1993, *Philadelphia* was released. It was the first mainstream Hollywood movie to speak out against homophobia and acknowledge HIV/AIDS. Tom Hanks won an Academy Award for his performance, and Bruce Springsteen's "Streets of Philadelphia" also won an Oscar. Still, many gays and lesbians in the eighties and nineties feared revealing their sexuality to their parents and closest friends. And some were still grappling with the issue of their sexuality. It couldn't have been easy, Nico thought, for a twenty-two-year-old who had just been thrust into the spotlight alongside his father to admit to himself and others that he was gay.

"What are you thinking about?" Le Marec asked.

Nico set the photos of Jean-Baptiste on the table.

"His lover bit him on the shoulder."

"And?"

The door opened. "We've got a problem," Commander Charlotte Maurin said quietly.

Someone just turned on the fan.

14

On the Avenue Jean-Jaurès, there was a hostel with a view of the Parc de la Villette. Tourists rarely stayed there for more than two nights. The rooms were small, and the toilets were screwed to the shower stalls. Shoeboxes stacked high, a human hive. It was the kind of place most people were happy to forget. But the guests, the manager, and his employees would remember this day.

Police cars and officers were crowded around the entrance like bees around a pot of honey. An ambulance made a U-turn and drove off as Nico and Maurin got out of their car and walked toward the lobby. Captain Ayoub Mouman took them inside. Forty, married, and the father of three, he was a stalwart member of the force.

"It's on the fourth floor. Follow me," he said, starting up the stairs. "They're already there. The cleaning woman found him. The poor woman must have been terrified. The EMTs just left. There was nothing they could do."

The officers standing guard let them into the room.

Inside, the scene was stomach-turning. The victim lay on the bed in a pool of blood. What looked like quarts of blood.

"Florian Bonnet. A twenty-year-old student. He was studying philosophy at the Catholic Institute," Maurin said. "He's the one who booked the room."

"His attacker severed his carotid artery," Moumen said. "He died in less than a minute, like a pig drained of its blood. The same thing."

Moumen, whose parents had immigrated from Algeria, was a demonstrative and talkative officer, the exact opposite of the soft-spoken Maurin. Nico knew that Moumen often had his colleagues over for dinner, and his wife was known for her elaborate Middle-Eastern dishes and delicacies.

"From the moment he was stabbed, there was no hope for him. The paramedics said you would have had to pinch the artery against the spinal cord to stop the blood. Nobody knows how to do that. Poor kid."

Police officers were trained to describe the facts as objectively as possible. This allowed them to keep their composure. But reality always tripped them up. Florian Bonnet was lying on his stomach, with his pants and underwear around his ankles. The showerhead, ripped out of the wall and covered with blood, was between his legs.

Nico didn't need to ask. "He was raped," he said.

Florian Bonnet was just a kid. His large eyes were still open in shock.

Maurin pointed to a specific spot on his body. "Like the other one," she said.

There was a deep gash on the victim's left shoulder.

"We didn't find the flesh anywhere. He must have taken it with him. Just like with Mathieu Leroy."

The question hung in the air before Moumen said it out loud. "Think it's the same man?"

"The location and modus operandi present many similarities," Nico said. "We need to figure out his motives. I have my ideas, but I'll need to talk with Professor Vilars. I'll go with you to the autopsy."

In the autopsy room, Professor Vilars and her collaborators would begin the external exam with photographs and X-rays. Next, they would record height, weight, and other general measurements; physical characteristics such as eye and hair color; any scars, tattoos, and other markings; and ethnicity. They would look for the presence of lividity and whether it conformed with the position of the body at the time it was discovered. They would search for lesions and other wounds and comment on the state of all the body's orifices, as well as any posthumous decay—to determine the time of death. After enough blood was drawn for testing and possible countertesting in court, they would make large incisions, hunting for subcutaneous bruising, among other things.

As the autopsy got under way, the usually talkative Captain Ayoub Moumen wasn't saying a word. Attending this procedure wasn't something he was doing voluntarily. His boss had sent him without asking his opinion. Nico knew this. The captain had deliberately avoided the morgue since watching the autopsy of a child killed by a drunk driver. Maurin, however, had decided it was time for her officer to come to terms with it.

But Moumen wasn't the only one who was having trouble. Nico was seeing his own mother's face superimposed on the lifeless body on the stainless-steel table. He tried to force the vision out of his mind. "Do you think it's the same guy who killed Mathieu Leroy?" he asked.

"The traces left by the knife blade are similar in both cases," Vilars replied.

"And the shoulder wound?"

Nico was doing everything he could to concentrate on the victim. Damn, it was hot in here.

"He was very determined to cut away part of the shoulder. This was no accident."

Moumen swallowed. Otherwise, he was a marble statue.

"Why the shoulder?" Nico asked. His voice was getting hoarse.

"Tell me your theory," Professor Vilars said. "I'm the chief medical examiner. You're the sleuths. Let's each do our job."

Nico exhaled.

"What if he bit his victims and then wanted to destroy the evidence?" Nico ventured. "A bite could have been useful for a DNA swab or a cast to compare with a suspect's dental records."

"You may be onto something," Vilars said. "The killer could have bitten the man's shoulder and then cut the whole area away postmortem to leave no traces of evidence."

Vilars began the internal exam by opening the rib cage. Instead of a Y-incision, she made a single incision from the chin to the pubis. She prepared to dissect the soft tissues and muscles and remove the organs one by one from the tongue to the rectum to analyze any pathologies. The head would be next. Vilars would cut through the hairy scalp. Then the screech of her oscillating saw would fill the room. The examiner would examine the bony structures, the muscular masses, the meninges, the cerebrospinal fluid, and the cerebral arteries before extricating the brain in search of a hematoma or a hemorrhage.

Moumen was as pale as a leek.

"We'll let you get to work," Nico finally said. He was worried that his colleague might collapse.

Vilars glanced at the captain and nodded. "You've seen the important part. Go ahead. Both of you can leave. I'll send you the report when I'm done."

"His parents will have to identify the body," Nico said.

"I'll be here."

"Thank you, Armelle."

Moumen had already dashed off.

15

"I have a theory about the killer's ritual," Nico said quickly. "The Butcher of Paris—that's what the reporters are calling him—cuts away part of the left shoulder of his victims because he's bitten them but doesn't want to leave any trace evidence."

Gathered in his office, Claire Le Marec, Jean-Marie Rost, David Kriven, and Charlotte Maurin were listening.

"There's a sexual component to this act," he added.

"Have you talked with Dominique Kreiss?" Le Marec asked.

"I've just called her. She's coming."

"Good idea," Kriven said. Nico stifled a smile. Kreiss had gently suggested that he consider working on his marriage, and even though Kriven had agreed that he loved his wife and would take to heart the psychologist's advice, he still had a crush on Kreiss. No harm, no foul.

Kreiss came in, greeted everyone, and took a seat at the table with the others.

"Bites are most commonly associated with murder and sexual-assault cases," she began. "We also see it in child-abuse cases. Some well-known serial killers, including Ted Bundy, have bitten their victims. A killer who bites tends to enjoy degrading his victim. He may pick any fleshy part of the body, such as the buttocks or the stomach. A female victim is often bitten on the breast or the inside of her thighs. When it's a man preying on another man, the biting most frequently occurs on the back, arms, shoulders, face, or scrotum. Fritz Haarmann, also known as the Butcher of Hanover, murdered his male victims by biting them on the neck. Coincidentally, female killers have been known to bite, although it's not as common. Stephanie Lazurus, a former Los Angeles police detective, bit her ex-lover's new girlfriend before killing her."

"Were the victims in these two new slayings gay?" Kriven asked.

"Yes, it appears that both of them were," Maurin said.

"There's actually some news about that," Rost said. "This was online at SOS Homophobia, the antihomophobia association."

He pulled a piece of paper out of his folder and put it on the table. Everyone leaned over to read it. "Safety alert—Parc de la Villette—Paris: SOS Homophobia has received reports of knife attacks in the Parc de la Villette and its immediate environs. Two have died. We ask people in the area to be extremely vigilant and to report anything suspicious to authorities. If you've been assaulted, call our hotline, or contact us through our website."

"I don't understand. Are we talking about an attacker who's homophobic or an attacker who's gay?" Kriven asked.

"It's not so clear-cut," Dominique Kreiss replied.

"Then explain it to us, please," said Nico.

"The number of homophobic attacks against young people has been high these past few years. We like to believe that society is more tolerant today, that mores have changed. But unfortunately, homophobia is ingrained and difficult to root out. Some people justify it on religious grounds. Some people are more clinical, if you will, about it and call homosexuality 'deviant.' Even people who claim they are tolerant and don't have a problem with homosexuality often still say they don't want to see it flaunted. Homophobia, therefore, is easy for many people to rationalize. They really see GLBT choices as something that's wrong and feel superior to gays and lesbians. It's interesting to note that studies have shown that homophobia correlates inversely with education and is more commonly a rural phenomenon than an urban one. It seems to be more pervasive among old people, especially older men. But the majority of homophobes who commit violent crimes against homosexuals appear to be young, violent, and socially adrift."

"So is it your opinion that the killer—or killers—is a homophobe who's out to get gays, or should we be looking for someone else, perhaps a gay guy who's just into killing other gays for whatever reason?" Kriven asked.

"I'm thinking that a garden-variety homophobe who's violent wouldn't be prone to biting," Kreiss said. "At the same time, a homophobic murderer who's repressing his own gay sexual orientation could very well bite during the commission of his crime. And let's remember, crimes of passion take place between gay lovers, just as they do between heterosexual couples. Biting could be involved in these instances, too. Biting signifies a release of tension. I'm sorry, Commander Kriven, at this point, I can't really answer your question."

"At any rate, we'll have to put out feelers in the gay community," Jean-Marie Rost said. "We may find some leads in ACT UP, SOS Homophobia, or other groups."

"Two murders in two nights," Claire Le Marec said. "Mathieu Leroy and Florian Bonnet."

"He's in high gear," Kreiss said.

"It's highly likely that our killer could attack again tonight," Rost said.

"We need to find out why these men were murdered," Nico said. "And do their homicides have anything to do with Jean-Baptiste Cassian's death? He had at least one gay encounter, and his fiancée discovered a bite on his shoulder, his left shoulder. I've confirmed it. The banquet was excavated, and his skeleton was found. Now young men of a similar age with similar physical characteristics are being attacked in the same area, most likely bitten on the left shoulder before being killed."

"You've got your work cut out for you. You could wind up falling on your ass," Michel Cohen had told him right before the meeting. "Or you'll pull it off, and I'll award you one of my Havanas." Fat chance it'll ever get smoked, Nico said to himself.

16

Once again, Nico and Caroline stopped at the nurses' station, where Anya's caregiver for the evening was stationed behind a computer monitor.

"Good evening, Chief Sirsky and Dr. Dalry," she said. "How are you?"

"We're fine, but more important, how is Mrs. Sirsky?"

"Her heart rate is still high, and her blood pressure is low. Same as last night. Her Glasgow reading is thirteen over fifteen, which is good."

Nico and Caroline thanked the nurse and went in to see Anya. Any semblance of calm started to crumble as soon as Nico laid eyes on her. She had the panicked look of a hunted-down animal. Nico wanted to yell and break the machines that sequestered his mother. But he smiled and rubbed her hand gently. Anya gripped it with all the strength she had left.

Caroline and Dr. Fursac had reminded Nico that his mother's reactions proved that her brain function hadn't been damaged. The Glasgow reading underscored that opinion. And Dr. Fursac had told him that they might soon be able to extubate her and transfer her to a step-down unit. That was good news.

"Try not to worry, *Maman*," he said. "You've been sick, but you're getting better. I have faith in you."

Anya seemed to cling to his words as though they were a lifeline.

"You know what they're telling me? That you've got an angel on your shoulder. Keep fighting, and soon we can free you of all this stuff. You deserve to have a room upstairs with a view."

His mother's eyes shone with hope.

"Stay strong, *Maman*. Okay?"

She nodded imperceptibly. But Nico could still read fear in her eyes. She had a tube in her trachea that had to make her feel like she was suffocating. And she had been strapped down, because the nurses thought she might pull out her tube and IV line.

Nico kissed her on her forehead. She closed her eyes, clearly exhausted and despondent.

Caroline put her head on his shoulder. He breathed in her scent.

"Let's go back home," she said.

She led him outside, away from the world of suffering and anguish, away from the hospital. Nico needed to be back at his place, curled up with Caroline. To make love to her, to feel relieved of his cares, if only for a few moments.

17

Laurence Clavel, the general director of the Parc de la Villette, let Nico and Jacques Langier, the former minister of culture, meet in her office.

"It's a very sad thing," the former minister said as he settled into the couch. "I consider Samuel Cassian a friend."

"You backed the project, right?" Nico asked.

"Project is the word for it. Samuel presented his idea to the president and me, and we were both absolutely taken by it. The Nouveau Realisme movement was brilliant—Yves Klein, Arman, Daniel Spoerri, Jean Tinguely, César Baldaccini, Niki de Saint Phalle. None of them were lacking in humor or a willingness to provoke. When Samuel suggested the Parc de la Villette, we were all the more intrigued."

"Was there any opposition back then?"

"Oh sure, there was a fuss. Planning the first archaeological excavations of modern art—people thought it was so avant-garde. But the idea fascinated us. It forced us to think about what would remain of our society, what people would remember, and what would have meaning to those who did the excavation thirty years after the burial."

"I'm guessing that not all of the cultural and scientific elite shared your enthusiasm."

"The conservatives were scathing, but they were very much a minority. Samuel was struggling with the issue of longevity. He wanted to know if his work would be recognized long after his celebrity had faded. Honestly, we all wonder if what we do will be remembered. We're all looking for some kind of immortality, don't you think?"

"Yes, I agree. Do you think any of the project's critics went too far?"

"Not really."

"Did anyone seem to be overly jealous?"

"There's always someone, but nobody comes to mind."

"Did you know Cassian's son, Jean-Baptiste?"

"Of course. He was a nice boy with plenty of talent. He disappeared, as you know. Samuel never really got over it."

"You weren't there at the start of the dig, I'm told."

"No, I had a prior obligation that I couldn't cancel. I promised Samuel that I would visit the site at a future date. Considering everything that's happened there, I guess I won't be doing that."

"I fear not. You should know that we've completed our preliminary investigation and have confirmed that the bones found in the pit belonged to a young man killed by a blow to the head thirty years ago."

Jacques Langier leaned forward.

"Jean-Baptiste?"

"It's him. We've confirmed it."

"Oh no! Poor Samuel."

"You didn't notice anything unusual during the banquet, did you? Anything about the father or the son?"

"I congratulated Jean-Baptiste on his success in New York. I still remember the odd smile he gave me. He didn't seem as happy as he usually was. He said that living was sometimes much messier than putting together an art show."

"Was he in some kind of trouble?"

"I couldn't tell you. To most people, he seemed like an easygoing young man with a promising future."

"Could his success have sparked some resentment from another artist?"

"He was twenty-two. He hadn't been on the scene all that long, certainly not long enough to make someone jealous enough to murder the boy!"

"He was seated at his father's right at the banquet, so he was, in essence, his father's second-in-command."

"Samuel Cassian was symbolically burying his entire oeuvre. It seems perfectly understandable that he'd want his son by his side."

"But maybe not everybody felt that way."

"I didn't hear anybody raise any objections at the lunch."

"Several pictures were taken to immortalize the event. Do you know who the photographer was? Was he perhaps a photographer from a newspaper or magazine?"

"I did see a photographer, but I have no idea who he was. He was seated near Samuel Cassian during the meal. And then he was busy taking the photos."

Nico had gotten as much from the man as he was going to get, at least for the moment. He stood up and thanked the minister of culture.

Langier also stood up. "Is it true that you've asked that the banquet be excavated in its entirety?" he asked.

"There's no way around it in a criminal investigation of this sort," Nico said.

"Well then, I'm sure you'll be able to count on Samuel's help. He'll do everything in his power to see to it that his son's grave is disinterred as respectfully as possible. He'd even be willing to sacrifice his work. Samuel is passionate about his artistic legacy, but his son's memory is far more important."

Samuel Cassian's heart and soul were now in that pit, where his son's body had been discarded years before. Nico wondered if that kind of abyss, where a parent's heart and soul sank after the loss of a child, could have a bottom. He was a father, and he never wanted to know the answer.

Before leaving the Pavillon Janvier, Nico went to see the archivist. Her office smelled of fresh paint. The finish on the floor looked just-done.

"Could you tell me who photographed Samuel Cassian's banquet thirty years ago?"

"I should have that information somewhere."

The archivist opened a drawer in her bookcase, took several folders out, selected one, and set it on a table.

"Damien Forest, a photographer for Reuters news service," she said.

"Thank you. How long have you been working here?"

"For quite some time now. I was hired to maintain the files during the park's construction. My job was supposed to end when the park opened, but I wound up with a long-term contract. The reactions when I tell people that I work at La Villette haven't changed since the day I was hired. They always say, 'Oh, the abattoirs' and then, 'Oh right, the Cité des Sciences.' I hope this incident won't damage the park's reputation. We've been trying to change the preconceptions for so long now."

Clearly, she was in love with the park she'd devoted so many years to.

"If you want to understand the place, I recommend Georges Franju's *Blood of the Beasts*. It's a documentary he made in 1948. It's weird, but honest and actually moving."

Nico made a mental note of it.

It was one o'clock. He went through the revolving door of Au Boeuf Couronné, a temple to meat and a last reminder of La Villette's famed artisans. It was a unique restaurant on the Avenue Jean-Jaurès, filled with the buzz typical of Parisian brasseries. Prim waiters made their way around the tables, their arms loaded with heavy plates, which they set down on white tablecloths.

Kriven raised his arm. Nico headed toward the table set for four. Rost and Plassard had just sat down. It wasn't often that they had the opportunity to eat together.

"Have you ordered yet?"

"We were waiting for you. You're the boss!"

The menu was a meat lover's dream.

"Should we get our own dishes or share?" Franck Plassard asked.

According to the menu, the *chateaubriand des bidochards* and the grilled rib of beef were enough for two people.

Clearly delighted, Kriven and Plassard looked through the selections and leaned together to discuss the various options.

"Look at the two of you—nothing but food on your minds," Nico said.

"The *pavé des mandataires* cut from the fillet looks like my thing," Kriven said.

"Good choice," Plassard chimed in.

"Just a gentle kiss on the grill is enough," Kriven said.

"We're in no position to be squeamish about blood," Rost said. "Let's order and be done with it."

"Yes, good idea," Nico said.

They settled on four *Fort des Halles* sirloin steaks, along with fluffy potatoes that the assistant headwaiter called absolutely extraordinary. And water, of course.

"How have the interviews been going?" Nico asked, buttering a slice of bread.

"No luck yet," Rost said.

"Jacques Langier told me that Jean-Baptiste Cassian didn't seem to be himself on the day of the banquet," Nico said, scooping up a forkful of potatoes. "Something was bothering him."

"None of the witnesses I spoke with said anything about that," Plassard replied.

"Let's look into it. But that's not what I'm most concerned about."

"Cassian cheating on his girlfriend?" Jean-Marie Rost asked. "Maybe Lara Krall wanted to get revenge."

"She would have needed help burying the body."

"Maybe Gregory Weissman was an accomplice?" the section chief suggested.

"They met each other much later. We'll need to verify that, of course. But I can't imagine her killing him with a hammer. And she seemed devastated by the news."

"Another thing: a photographer from Reuters was at the banquet. Somebody named Damien Forest. Bring him in."

"No problem," said Rost.

"Did you find anything from the names Samuel Cassian and Lara Krall gave us?"

Kriven cleared his throat. "They match, first of all. We found the couple's friends. Michel Géko is on Stiff Alley: a fatal car accident five years after Jean-Baptiste's disappearance. Jérôme Dufour has an art gallery in Lyon. Laurent Mercier is a landscape painter in Vincennes."

The waiter brought them their orders.

"Nathan Sellière works in antiques, and Daniel Vion is a draftsman."

Kriven cut into his steak and wolfed down a hunk with relish.

"Camille Frot is now Mrs. Mercier, all settled down. Sophie Bayle is a jewelry designer. She's done well for herself; her brand's pretty famous."

"Sophie Bayle's divorced. Dufour and the Merciers are married with children. Only Nathan Sellière and Daniel Vion are single, and we don't know their sexual orientation."

"Let's not be hasty," Nico said. "Marital status doesn't necessarily correlate with sexual orientation. We all know that. Further, we haven't determined that it's even a key factor. We need to remember what Dominique Kreiss told us."

"Should we call them in?" Kriven asked.

"Yes, give them the third degree, and see what happens. Jean-Baptiste was murdered, and I'm fairly certain he knew his murderer. His burial in the Parc de la Villette hardly seems like a coincidence."

"If it's Géko, we're too late," Plassard said.

"But in that case, Mathieu Leroy and Florian Bonnet wouldn't have been murdered," Nico pointed out.

"Maybe the murders aren't connected," Rost ventured.

Nico wondered if he was grasping at straws. Was he putting too much faith in his instincts? "We shouldn't rule out any possibilities, even if they're not concrete. But for now, let's put together as much information as we can on this group of friends. That's something to go on. And I want to find out who took those pictures of him."

They had finished their steaks and were scraping their plates.

"Cheese or dessert, gentlemen?" the waiter asked.

"Just a round of espresso for everyone," Nico said.

Nico walked back to his car at the Pavillon Janvier. He started driving, thinking about all the things that had happened in the past five days. He felt queasy. He had already lost his father. He wanted more time with Anya.

Then he looked around, astonished. He'd driven into the nineteenth arrondissement and was on the Rue de Crimée, by the Parc des Buttes-Chaumont.

His childhood. Saint Serge Russian Orthodox Church, 93 Rue de Crimée. He had attended weekly services with Tanya and their mother. Nico parked in front of a hair and nail salon and a restaurant called La Maison d'Arganier. The Franprix grocery store was still where it had always been. Its window display looked unchanged.

A rusty gate at number 93 didn't inspire much confidence. Was the church still open? His heart beating, Nico slipped into an uninviting alley. He couldn't stop thinking of his younger self trotting ahead as his mother held Tanya's hand and scolded him to stay with them.

At the end of the alley, where the trash cans stood, a pinkish house was surrounded by taller buildings. A boat adrift in a harbor filled with ocean liners. As he got closer, Nico felt a long-forgotten sensation—of entering a different time and place, of being transported to a peaceful haven thousands of miles from Paris and everyday life.

To the left of the house, a stone path zigzagged up a hill. Nico walked past a garage turned into a bookstore and a crumbling mansion. Higher up was a sort of bunker: the Saint Serge Institute of Theology, founded in 1925, the only Russian Orthodox school of higher education in the city. Through the open windows, he could hear someone reciting a litany in a low voice. Nico shivered as he walked slowly, afraid of being discovered. Then he looked at the top of the hill.

The church was a lost gem. It looked like a mountain chalet on the outside, but it was a pure neo-Gothic church designed by Dimitry Stelletsky. The interior was absolutely spellbinding. All Orthodox churches had a contemplative atmosphere complemented by frescoes, gilded statues, icons, candlelight, and incense. Nico smiled; he and his sister remembered the silliest things every bit as much as they remembered the Byzantine hymns that had bewitched them.

"Nico?" came a voice behind him.

He jumped, his daydream forgotten.

"Is that you, Nico?"

Nico turned. The parish priest he had known as a child was standing there. He was a large man with a thick beard and hair that was still brown. He looked as though he had come straight from the Russian steppes.

"I haven't seen you in such a long time," the priest said, his voice echoing in the church.

Nico didn't know how to reply. Between his Catholic father and his Orthodox mother, the Great Schism of 1054 had played out in his family. But even though Anya had won and had brought up Tanya and him in the Russian Orthodox Church—probably because his father wasn't a regular churchgoer anyway—he never felt as though he legitimately belonged.

The priest set one hand on Nico's shoulder. With his free hand, he shook Nico's.

"It's good to see you, Nico. And your sister, how is she doing? I've missed you both."

Nico still couldn't say a word. There were too many emotions.

"Let's sit down and talk," the priest said with a smile. "Tell me how your mother is. I know you need to talk about her. I do, too."

So he knew. And if he did, so did the rest of Paris's Russian community. Nico let the priest lead him to a pew. He wished Tanya could be there with him. He wanted Caroline, too. These two, along with Anya and his niece, Lana—short for Milana, which meant "beloved" in Russian—were the four most important women in his life. He didn't want to lose any of them.

18

"Her heart rate and blood pressure are normal," Dr. Fursac was telling Nico, Caroline, and Alexis. "We've extubated her. Her Glasgow reading is fifteen over fifteen, meaning she has good eye, verbal, motor responses. And there are no signs of infection. All in all, she's presenting well. But we've noted some erratic heart rhythms on the EKG, so we'll need to pay attention to that. Your mother will be transferred to a step-down unit tomorrow morning."

Caroline and Alexis agreed that this was good news. Her heart was still a concern, but they had to savor every victory and thank the heavens that Anya was alive.

Dr. Fursac led them to Anya's bed. Nico and Caroline stood on one side. Tanya and Alexis stood on the other.

"My children," Anya said in a shaky voice after looking them over.

She didn't have to say anything else.

19

"Lara Krall and her husband, Gregory Weissman, met several years after Jean-Baptiste Cassian's death," Kriven said without preamble.

The commander had been waiting for Nico to arrive on this Saturday morning and joined him in his office as soon as the chief had poured his coffee. At La Crim', there weren't any vacations or weekends off when they were on the trail of a killer or killers.

Nico added Kriven's latest piece of information to his mental file. Was Jean-Baptiste's slaying linked to the two recent murders? Nico had a hunch—which Kriven seemed to share—but so far there was no hard evidence.

"There does seem to be a connection, if only because of the sexual orientation of the three young men," Kriven said.

For the moment, however, Nico wanted to focus on the Jean-Baptiste murder.

"I never really suspected Lara Krall," he said. "It wasn't likely that she'd kill her fiancé and bury him in a public park. We should focus on Jean-Baptiste's friends. If anyone can give us more clues about the victim and his relationships, it'll be one of them."

"I interviewed Sylvia Bayle and Nathan Sellière yesterday afternoon."

"The jewelry designer and the antiques dealer?"

"Yes. They didn't know who took those photos of Jean-Baptiste. And they'd never heard of Damien

Forest, that Reuters photographer who covered the banquet-performance."

"How did they react when you told them that Jean-Baptiste had experienced at least one gay encounter?"

"It didn't really surprise Sylvia Bayle."

"No? Why not?"

"Jean-Baptiste loved Lara. That was clear to her. But when she looked back on it, she realized that they seemed more like siblings or friends than lovers. With girls, he was always the protective, playful brother. Sylvia Bayle came to believe that deep down, Jean-Baptiste was attracted to men."

Nico took a sip of his coffee.

"So what if Jean-Baptiste had more than a one-time fling?" Kriven ventured. "What if he was involved in a serious—and secret—relationship?"

"With the person who took those portraits of Jean-Baptiste?" Nico asked.

"Why not? These shots do give the impression of intimacy."

"What did you think of Nathan Sellière?"

"He's far more interested in antiques than the fairer sex or Cassian's escapades. He's a bit on the fat side, and he seems to sweat a lot. But he's got a good mind for business, I'm told. In the antiques community, he has a reputation for emptying pockets. He's done quite well for himself."

"That wouldn't seem to line up with our picture of the Parc de la Villette murderer. Being attractive and in good shape would be important to that sort of seducer, I imagine."

"Yes, but I don't agree entirely. Nathan Sellière's money might attract a few people."

"True, but according to Charlotte, Mathieu Leroy and Florian Bonnet weren't looking for partners. Economic stability is sometimes a factor when you're looking for a mate. But it appears that Leroy and Bonnet were just two men who liked to go out and have a good time."

"At any rate, I'm interviewing the Merciers, Jérôme Dufour, and Daniel Vion today."

"No news of Damien Forest?"

"Not yet. We're working on it."

"We'll come back to that later."

"That's fine."

"Speaking of problems, I've noticed that you haven't been as sharp these past few days. I'm concerned."

Kriven frowned. "You've had a lot on your own mind."

"David, don't. I've seen all too well how hard things have been with Clara."

"She's had trouble getting back on her feet. We don't talk much, you know."

"So are you thinking about getting involved in a new relationship?"

"Dominique and I are just friends!" Kriven said, tensing up.

"Take my advice, David. You love Clara. Don't give up on your marriage just yet."

"Dominique gave me the same advice."

"That proves she's a smart woman. She hasn't tried to take advantage of the situation, even though I'm sure you're her type."

Kriven smiled.

"Tell Clara what you know in your heart to be true. She's a good woman, David. You two deserve a bit of good luck. God knows, we have enough of the other kind to go around."

The police commander stared at his feet. "I'll do that," he said at last.

"You'd better!" Nico smiled.

Kriven left to find his team in the Coquibus room.

The phone rang. Nico picked up the receiver.

"Hello, old buddy!"

Few people had Nico's direct line. It was Alexandre Becker, a friend and also a magistrate. Nico and Becker's professional collaborations had always made the higher-ups look good. So Becker was frequently assigned to Nico's cases.

"The prosecutor has opened a criminal investigation to determine the date and exact cause of Jean-Baptiste Cassian's death, and I've just been given the case. So here I am, once again a slave to La Crim'," Becker said with a chuckle.

"We all know you love it."

"You got that right. Okay, I've read the preliminary report. I imagine there are further developments, and you have updates to share?"

"That's right."

"Do you have a few minutes to fill me in?"

"I'll come over."

The Palais de Justice occupied a third of the Île de la Cité island. It was a sanctuary of law encompassing the police headquarters, government administrative offices, a jail, and the courthouse. This structure symbolized the splendor of the French Republic, with its gilded embellishments, three-sided courtyard, and large stone staircase leading to the vestibule flanked by four monumental statues that allegorized strength, abundance, justice, and prudence.

Getting to Magistrate Alexandre Becker's office from headquarters at 36 Quai des Orfèvres didn't take all that long. But it was still a feat. Nico trotted down Stairwell A to the second floor and made his way through the door that opened directly to the courts and their offices. A tiled hallway, with uncomfortable benches on one side and offices on the other, led to the lawyers' library, which boasted a monumental wooden door. Then the corridor narrowed until it was nothing more than a passageway. The main part of the building was a few steps ahead. Nico crossed an immense span of marble floor interspersed with statues, bronze busts, and columns. Outside the windows, he could see the royal Sainte-Chapelle chapel and its ancient windows, which were perfect examples of religious architecture dating to the Middle Ages.

He entered the René Parodi vestibule. A long hallway stretched ahead, ending at Stairwell F and the investigating magistrates. He preferred Stairwell G, which was more discreet. Becker worked on the fourth floor. To reach it, Nico had to get through a locked door. He entered the numbers on a keypad. Nico held out his badge to the guard, a tense, Sylvester Stallone look-alike, and knocked on the magistrate's door. One day he'd have to bring a timer.

"Nice of you to come all the way over here," Becker said.

The two of them met more often in Nico's office. "Have a seat," Becker said as he took out a notepad and a pen. "I ordered the excavation of the full 130 feet of the banquet. The heavy equipment's there already, and Professor Queneau's at the helm."

"What does the Society for the Disinterment of the *Tableau-Piège* say?"

"Its directors understand what we're trying to do and are working with us to ensure that their aims are still met."

"And Samuel Cassian?"

"It looks like he'll be involved, as you guessed. All right, let's start with the discovery of the skeleton."

Nico summarized the investigation, including the interviews with Lara Krall and the victim's group of friends. He mentioned Damien Forest, the banquet photographer, and laid out the pictures of the younger Cassian.

"They're very nice photos."

"That's what's bothering me," Nico said.

"They're better than ordinary amateur photos. And they show a certain intimacy."

Nico summoned his courage and took the plunge.

"Here's how I see things. We're looking for Damien Forest. I think Jean-Baptiste Cassian was gay or bi and in the closet. We're questioning Jean-Baptiste's friends on that aspect of his life. I'm wondering if the person who took these photographs was Jean-Baptiste's lover and if one of his friends knows who that person is."

"You're setting aside the idea that someone was jealous of the father's celebrity or his son's? Jealous enough to murder Jean-Baptiste?"

"Absolutely not. Kriven's group is still questioning everyone who was at the banquet and the excavation. We're trying to get at any enmities. But my gut tells me that artistic jealousy wasn't the motive. I want to focus on the group closest to the victim. One of his friends could match our profile of the Butcher of Paris and—"

Becker stood up, a pensive look on his face. "So you really think that the person who murdered Jean-Baptiste could be the one who murdered these two other young men? That's a big leap."

"Think about it. As soon as he's exhumed from the *tableau-piège*, Mathieu Leroy and Florian Bonnet are killed in the same area. One in the Leitner Cylinder, the other in a hotel room that overlooks the park. It's a strange coincidence, isn't it? We're dealing with attacks that appear to be homosexual in nature in the area where the bones of a promising and probably gay young artist were found."

"Don't you think you're being a little hasty, calling Cassian gay? He was about to get married."

"Precisely!"

Alexandre Becker raised his eyebrows.

"Maybe we should be looking for a scorned lover who didn't like the fact that he was about to get married," Nico said.

"That's a lot of gut feeling, don't you think?"

"I may be skipping some steps here, but it's plausible, isn't it?"

Nico noticed that he'd raised his voice, and his breathing had become shallow. He paused. An image of Anya with monitors attached to her chest flashed in his mind. He looked away from Becker for a moment and took a deep breath.

"There's something else," Nico told Becker. "Lara Krall found bite marks on her fiancé's shoulder. It sparked an argument between the two of them. And I think the murderer in the Parc de la Villette is biting his victims in the same spot and then cutting away that part of their flesh to avoid leaving any evidence. Leroy and Bonnet are the spitting image of Jean-Baptiste Cassian."

Becker was silent for a few minutes. It felt like an eternity to Nico.

"Fine," Becker said at last. "The prosecutor has not opened the criminal investigation of the Leroy and Bonnet cases, but it can't wait any longer."

"If you can, give her a push."

"I will. In any event, I imagine you don't have an alternative scenario?"

"Whether or not the recent park murders are related, I believe that Jean-Baptiste and the person who murdered him were very close. So it's crucial that we keep exploring that lead."

"Hmm," Becker said. "And how is your mother?"

Nico looked him in the eye. "The whole thing with my mother has shaken me up, you're right. But I'm still running the show."

Becker was almost a brother. He had lost his mother when he was seven years old, and his wife, Stephanie, had been calling Caroline every day to ask for the latest news on Anya. Of all his friends, Becker was in the best position to understand how distraught he was.

Nico got up, and the two men hugged.

"She'll be all right, Nico. Don't worry."

Nico returned to his office. He needed to think. He recalled the archivist's recommendation and searched online for Franju's *Blood of the Beasts*. He started the video and turned up the sound.

The camera moved from a bucolic setting to the slaughterhouses. Nico glimpsed the Porte de Pantin and the market at La Villette. The Canal de l'Ourcq marked the boundary between the two worlds. The animals were unloaded at the abattoirs, and the workers, with cigarettes hanging from their lips, severed the animals' spinal cords before bleeding them. The steaming blood flowed into containers or streamed down drains. Then the butchers skinned the animals, removed their feet, and carved them up. The words underscored the violence and odd lyricism of the images.

Nico lost the thread for a few moments. He was thinking about Marcel, who was in charge of the human bodies donated to the medical and dental programs at Paris Descartes University. Marcel had once been a butcher at La Villette. He was an incredible man, and Nico visited him often. Marcel had told him how the workers at the abattoirs labored at frenetic speeds under harsh conditions. The jobs were highly specialized. There were slaughterers, carvers, and meat carriers. Some jobs, such as removing bristles and fat, were reserved for women.

Nico was pensive, his mind fixated on La Villette's atmosphere. He understood why Samuel Cassian had chosen the northern half of the park—the half with the abattoirs, the City of Blood—to bury his banquet-performance. It went hand in glove with the artistic and scientific auspices of the place. Cassian had been ruminating on the idea of death.

"Nico?"

The voice jolted Nico out of his torpor. Kriven was in the doorway.

"It's about Damien Forest, the photographer from Reuters."

"Yes?"

"The agency had nothing on him. He never worked for them. So I did some more research. Damien Forest never existed. There isn't any trace of him anywhere."

20

Daniel Vion was the last of Jean-Baptiste Cassian's close friends to be interviewed. He had taken all the group photos, but "didn't like being in front of the camera," as Lara Krall had put it.

Nico and Kriven met him in a small interview room on the top floor at headquarters. Vion was a well-dressed man who certainly didn't look fifty-two years old. Nico could see right away that he spent time and money on his appearance. He probably used only the most expensive products on his neatly trimmed hair and beard. His clothes, meanwhile, were stylish without being trendy. The term "metrosexual" popped into Nico's head. These days, it seemed, all men—from truck drivers to male models—were paying attention to their looks.

Commander Kriven set out the group photos taken thirty years earlier. He and Nico had decided to pull out all the stops.

"They're yours, aren't they?" Kriven asked evenly.

Vion slowly went over the pictures. He was smiling. "Where did you find these? I haven't seen them in years. They bring back such good memories."

"You're not answering my question," Kriven replied calmly.

"Oh, of course I took these. But you already knew that."

So he was arrogant.

"Do you remember who these people were?" Kriven asked.

Kriven would do all the talking. Nico would watch. Vion had been quick to act surprised by the photos. He knew he was being sized up, and his annoyance and anxiety would intensify. It was also very warm in this room, under the zinc shingles, and the bars on the windows accentuated the jail-like feeling of the space.

"There's Sophie."

"Sophie who?"

"Bayle, I think. And here's Camille Frot. She married Laurent, who's over here in this photo. These people are Mr. and Mrs. Mercier. Hmm. Oh, Nathan! That's him. Nathan Sellière. They hung out with him. They used to go to his place all the time."

It looked like an act to Nico. He was sure the man knew he wasn't at some children's show.

"Lara Krall, the happiest one," Vion said. "She was engaged to Jean-Baptiste Cassian. And there's Jérôme Dufour. If I remember correctly, he's living in Lyon now. He owns a gallery. Michel, though, died in a car accident. Such a shame. Michel Géko, right there. Géko."

Kriven slowly set the portraits of Jean-Baptiste Cassian on the table, one after another.

"Good memories," Kriven said in a perfect imitation. "Are these yours?"

Daniel Vion frowned and shook his head.

"I do group photos and trips. That's what I'm good at. I don't do portraits. The person who took these photos is more talented than I am."

"Damien Forest, does that name mean anything to you?"

"Never heard of him."

"He's a photographer," Kriven said.

"Did he take these pictures?" Vion asked.

"If it wasn't you…"

"You should ask Lara. She'd know better than I would."

"You went to the École des Beaux-Arts with her and Jean-Baptiste, didn't you? Were you good friends?"

"We spent a few wonderful years there."

"Then you went your separate ways."

"Jean-Baptiste's disappearance split us up. Lara had a hard time with it and became pretty isolated. And we each had our own paths to follow. You know how that is. Life."

"But you've stayed in touch. Otherwise you wouldn't have known about Géko's death, or the Merciers' marriage, or Jérôme Dufour's work in Lyon."

"That's true. I went to Camille and Laurent's wedding. We call each other once or twice a year, around Christmastime."

"Do all of you in this group still talk to each other?"

"Oh sure. We were passionate about our art, and just about all of us are still involved in it in one way or another. Sophie makes jewelry. Jérôme has his gallery. Nathan is an antiquarian. The Merciers have built their place for landscape painters, and I'm a draftsman."

"What about Lara?"

"She gave all that up."

"Because her fiancé left her?"

"That would be understandable."

"At the time of his disappearance, did you think that he had simply left of his own accord?"

Daniel Vion sighed.

"Nobody knew for sure," he said. "Jean-Baptiste's mother claimed that he had gone to live in the United States."

"Did she tell you that?"

As he talked, Vion had been glancing at Nico and fidgeting. The chief knew his silence was making the man uncomfortable.

"No, Jérôme Dufour told me that."

"Are you happy with your work as a drafter?" Kriven asked. He had switched the subject to make Vion even more uncomfortable. In addition, he had deliberately called Vion a drafter, instead of a draftsman, to suggest that he didn't have much regard for the profession.

"It's the profession I wanted to be in. After graduating from the École des Beaux-Arts, I went to the Paris Design Institute. I work in a design firm that has well-known corporate clients. Do the names Alcatel and Salomon mean anything to you?"

"Do you do everything on the computer?" Kriven asked with the same determination to belittle the master draftsman.

"It's how things are done today. That's all. But the work has lost none of its creativity. In fact, digital design has allowed us to be even more imaginative than we could be with drawing pens and paper."

"Do you know why you're here, Mr. Vion?" Nico finally asked.

The man jumped. He didn't return Nico's gaze and tried to fixate on Kriven, who was as immobile as stone.

"Do you know why you're here, Mr. Vion?" Nico repeated, his voice raised.

"They told me you were reopening the investigation into Jean-Baptiste's disappearance."

"You haven't heard anything about the excavation of Samuel Cassian's *tableau-piège*? Or the skeleton that was found in the pit? Do you not read the papers, Mr. Vion?"

"I do. But what does any of that have to do with me?"

He was trembling now and had lost all traces of his arrogance.

"Did you know that Jean-Baptiste was unfaithful to Lara Krall while they were engaged?" Nico said.

Astonishment was plain on Daniel Vion's face.

"And that he had cheated on her with a man?"

"I… No! I had no idea."

"You're a bachelor yourself. Is that a lifestyle choice, Mr. Vion?"

Nico hated going down this path, but his hand had been forced.

"I had a companion for several years."

"And now?"

"I'm single, and I'm happy."

"Would you call yourself a ladies' man, Mr. Vion?"

"I don't see why that concerns you," he shot back.

He was sweating bullets and stammering.

"Do you share Jean-Baptiste's preferences?"

Vion turned pale. He was hyperventilating.

"If you must know, I have had relationships with women and men."

Fundamentally, this didn't bother Nico. In ancient Greece and Rome, bisexuality was socially acceptable. It was common among Chinese emperors and the shoguns of Japan. Nearly half of the men Alfred Kinsey studied had engaged in sexual relations with both men and women. Even Sigmund Freud claimed that humans were basically bisexual—although Nico thought that was going a little too far. He didn't really care to snoop in anyone else's bedroom. But it was possible that Daniel Vion's sexual orientation had a bearing on this case.

"Were you attracted to Jean-Baptiste?"

"He was a friend! And he was engaged to Lara."

"But he was cheating on her. Did you have a lovers' quarrel?"

"No, no, and no! I didn't know anything about this and certainly not that he was cheating on Lara!"

"Where do you find your men, Daniel? Do you go to bars to meet your lovers?"

"I don't need to!"

"What's your type? Younger guys?"

"What exactly are you accusing me of? Pedophilia?"

"I'm thinking of men around Jean-Baptiste's age. You must miss him terribly. Enough that you're looking for him in your prey."

"That's horrible."

"Which you could say about Jean-Baptiste, who was struck in the head with a hammer thirty years ago before being thrown in his father's banquet-performance pit. The bones there are his."

The room was quiet again. Nico scrutinized his suspect's eye movements.

Kriven broke the silence. "Where were you on Wednesday night, Mr. Vion? That was the night Florian Bonnet was killed. He's the second victim of the Butcher of Paris."

"I was home!" Vion spluttered. "What are you suggesting?"

"And the night before? Tuesday night?"

He stared at them wide-eyed, silent.

"We'll need to see your planner, Mr. Vion."

"Why?"

"Because these murders were committed in the vicinity of the banquet-performance, and they may have a connection to Jean-Baptiste Cassian's disappearance," Nico said.

"I didn't have anything to do with those murders," Vion said weakly. He looked like an animal trapped in La Villette's dark abattoirs.

They were all seated around the table in Nico's office: Becker, Rost, Kriven, and Maurin.

"We've made a composite of Damien Forest's face, according to what the guests at the banquet remember," Rost said.

"The nonexistent Damien Forest," Becker pointed out.

"That's true," Kriven said. "But there was a photographer of some kind."

"I've contacted Samuel Cassian," Nico said. "I asked him how he picked the photographer. Oddly enough, he said his son chose the photographer. And Jean-Baptiste told him he was someone named Damien Forest, who worked for Reuters."

"And Lara Krall?" Alexandre Becker asked.

"I'll go see her with the composite sketch," Nico replied.

"It would be hard to positively ID someone from this drawing," Becker said. "Honestly, this guy looks like everybody and nobody. Not to mention he's thirty years older now."

"And it's worth noting that the sketch doesn't look like any of the victim's friends," Rost said.

"You'll have to show the banquet guests the old pictures that Daniel Vion took," Nico said. "Maybe one of them will recognize Damien Forest more easily than we can. David, see if you can get your hands on an old photo of Vion—I know he didn't like to have his picture taken, but there must be one somewhere—and mix it in with the others. I'll show the whole set to Jacques Langier, and you can do the same with Samuel Cassian."

"That's a good idea," Becker said. "We need to solve this mystery of who Damien Forest was."

"Let's not forget that Jean-Baptiste Cassian was the one who brought him in," Nico said.

"What did you learn when you interviewed his friends?" Becker asked.

"We had to push them a bit, especially the men," Kriven said. "If there's a wolf among the sheep, we have to use scare tactics and make him think he's a suspect. When a wolf senses that hunters are tracking him down, he'll do anything to save his skin."

"Anything concrete?"

"Two of them match our Butcher's profile," Nico said.
Everyone looked at him.

"Michel Géko is dead, so he doesn't count. Nathan Sellière is a bachelor, but according to David, he's not particularly interested in sex of any kind. Jérôme Dufour is a gallery owner in Lyon. He's married and has a teenager. A bit soft and posh. Physically, he'd fit, but he's definitely heterosexual, and he beds other women whenever he can."

"And if Dufour was in Lyon on the nights of the attacks, he's out of the running," Kriven said.

"So that leaves Laurent Mercier and Daniel Vion," Magistrate Becker said.

"Laurent Mercer married Camille, and they have three children. He built a landscape painters' place out in Vincennes. His wife works there part time. Daniel Vion is a draftsman at a design office in Paris. He's a confirmed bachelor and bisexual."

"I put together their profiles for Dominique Kreiss."

"Because we're combining the homicides, we'll have to verify their alibis for both Tuesday and Wednesday night," Becker said.

"Charlotte, you're in charge of that," Nico said. "I'd like the two of them to be brought in again. And let's ask forensics identification to help."

"According to the reports from the medical examiner's office and the forensics lab, the murderer was organized and smart," Becker said. "He didn't leave any evidence. Pretty interesting, considering the violence of his acts. You wouldn't think someone that crazed would have so much discipline."

"He allowed himself one bite on the shoulder, just as Jean-Baptiste Cassian's lover took only one bite," Nico said.

"You really are convinced that all of these murders are connected," Becker said.

Nico knew his men were behind him, and they wouldn't question him. But his theory still didn't have any real proof. And even though Becker and he were friends, he still needed to win him over.

"I suspect that the *tableau-piège* excavation and the skeleton's discovery shook up our man. The rage that drove him to kill Jean-Baptiste thirty years ago has re-surfaced. He feels the need to attack Jean-Baptiste again through the young men who resemble him. The two gay victims almost certainly were bitten on the shoulder, the same way Cassian was bitten. And the locations of the murders speak for themselves. It's too many coincidences. And it's possible that Damien Forest was Jean-Baptiste's boyfriend."

"That will have to be determined as quickly as possible," Becker said.

Jacques Langier happened to still be in Paris that Saturday because of a parliamentary committee meeting. He wouldn't be returning to his constituency until late in the evening. He'd been able to squeeze in a meeting with Nico at the National Assembly, which was mostly empty on the weekends.

Nico walked into the large building, a centerpiece of French history. During the workweek, it was like an ant-hill, with members of Parliament, assistants, employees, soldiers, police officers, and visitors streaming through. The austere colonnade hid nothing. Beyond the daily sessions, there were conferences to plan the week's schedule, as well as committee meetings, research meetings, and political meetings. The building also had its own post office, which handled millions of letters every year, a photo-copying room, and a monumental library where anybody could get newspapers, Internet access, or one of 750,000 books. The National Assembly was itself a city within the city, boasting restaurants, a barbershop, and an in-firmary. The president's entry to a parliamentary session, amid the Republican Guard's drumbeats, was well worth watching. Nico had seen it with Dimitri in the Galerie des Fêtes, followed by a session full of stormy debates.

At the entrance, near the three-sided courtyard, Nico held up his badge. Here, the security agents smiled, as long as you didn't give them trouble. Nico had locked up his automatic pistol at headquarters to avoid any difficulties. Although he was the Criminal Investigation Division's chief, people would have broken into a cold sweat if he'd been allowed in with a gun. It was a strange world, where anything was possible. So it wasn't acceptable for even high-ranking visitors to come in wearing a weapon.

The security officers gave Nico a visitor's badge and escorted him through the hallways to Jacques Langier's office.

"Come in, Chief," Langier said, smiling. "How's the investigation coming along?"

"It's starting to fall into place."

Langier waved to a chair where Nico could sit down. "What did you bring? Pictures?"

Nico handed them to Langier.

"Take a look at these faces. I'd like to know if you recognize Damien Forest, who was the photographer at the banquet."

For the third time in four days, Commander Kriven knocked on Samuel Cassian's door. The artist seemed to be doing better. Kriven felt strangely relieved; his wife had only her husband to rely on, and Kriven liked Mrs. Cassian. Maybe she had severe emotional problems, but she was a loving and wounded mother. Like Clara. Lately, he had been telling himself to have more patience with Clara. He could take inspiration from Samuel Cassian, who seemed to be dedicated to his wife. There was love to spare in this apartment.

The artist welcomed him warmly, and his wife brought out yet another plate of aperitifs. Samuel Cassian gave the commander a sly wink.

"A glass of white, young man?"

"With pleasure, sir."

His host served him.

"This is a 2005 grand cru Bâtard-Montrachet. We've moved from Côte Chalonnaise to Beaune. I'm a fan of Burgundy, as you've probably guessed. I hope you are too."

"I'm coming to enjoy it."

Samuel Cassian gave him a wry look.

"Well, that's one good thing to come out of this ordeal," Cassian said. "To what do I owe the pleasure of this visit, young man?"

Mrs. Cassian was watching, her eyes sparkling. Kriven hoped she wasn't waiting to hear that her son had been found in the United States. His hands started shaking.

"I have to show you a picture. I'd like to see if you recognize Damien Forest."

"Damien Forest?" Mrs. Cassian asked, surprised.

"I'll explain, my dear. Just you wait."

David held out the three-decades-old photo of Daniel Vion. The aging painter put on his glasses and furrowed his brow.

21

That Sunday, before going to the hospital, Nico decided to take Caroline and Dimitri out to lunch at the Paris-Moscou restaurant on the Rue Mauconseil in the first arrondissement. His mother loved this spot, which was a few steps from Les Halles and the Saint Eustache Cathedral. The food was a savory feast. Along the walls, all the Russian saints could be seen, as well as tableaus, trinkets, and Orthodox crosses. Dozens of *matryoshkas* in vivid colors were arrayed on a shelf. Here, the French music coming over the loudspeakers seemed quite out of place.

They ate eggplant caviar on toast as they waited for the traditional dishes of stuffed cabbage and turkey Kiev—an escalope rolled up with prunes and cheese. For dessert, they had *vatrushka*, a Danish pastry with farmer's cheese and raisins. Dimitri washed it down with soda, while the adults had Ukrainian beers. They raised their glasses to Anya's health. Dimitri was impatient to hug her, as he hadn't seen her since she'd fallen ill.

The hospital atmosphere was a stark contrast to that of the Paris-Moscou. Instead of the hearty Russian brews and vivid *matryoshkas*, the hospital offered gray tile, foreign smells, and the hushed talk of nurses and doctors. It annoyed Nico that a person had to be a doctor or a nurse to understand the lingo. Still, he found it reassuring that his mother was in a hospital with cutting-edge equipment and an extraordinarily qualified staff. Dimitri, on the other hand, was clearly intimidated by all the technical paraphernalia and was looking withdrawn.

Dr. Xavier Jondeau, the doctor on duty, came to meet them.

"Her blood pressure has risen, and her heart rate is high," he said. "But her oxygen saturation is normal. And the cerebral issues have been completely resolved. That's good news. We've seen ventricular extrasystoles with patients who've had ventricular tachycardia."

"They're ventricular contractions provoked by abnormal electrical discharges from the heart," Caroline translated. "That's why Anya keeps feeling palpitations and pain. If they recur, they can get worse."

"We'll have to run some tests before making more medical or surgical decisions," Dr. Jondeau said.

Another moment passed, and finally they were in Anya's room. She was so pale. Dimitri, however, brightened as soon as he saw her. He called her by her Russian name, and she responded in Russian, telling him how happy she was to see him.

"You scared us to death," Dimitri said in Russian. "Don't do it again, please."

Anya switched back to French. "Don't worry, my little angel. The doctors are going to fix me up."

Nico had never seen his mother look so fatigued. She turned to him. "Come here, my son. Give me a hug."

Nico tried to hold back his feelings. He clumsily worked his way around the beeping machine that was recording her vitals, her IV line, and the monitors attached to her chest and gently embraced her. Anya was so pale, and Nico could feel his anxiety rising. Neither Samuel Cassian nor Jacques Langier had been able to identify Damien Forest in the pictures. Nico had made a promise, and he still had his end to hold up.

22

The bathroom mirror reflected a handsome man. He pulled out his mascara, the sole bit of makeup that he allowed himself, to lengthen his eyelashes. The glam look accentuated his dark and shadowy gaze. It was provocative. The eyes and the naturally angelic smile were a winning combination. And the party was tonight. His libido was at full throttle.

Tight jeans, a black polo shirt, Italian leather shoes—Clément looked good. He slipped his wallet and a condom into his back pocket, grabbed the car keys, and shut the apartment door behind him. He wanted to drink water and dance the whole night, to just have a grand time. A few bumps, a few caresses, a deep kiss, and his desire would become uncontrollable. He would get laid tonight.

And if he was lucky, he'd find the right person. Maybe someone to actually spend time with, someone to see every day. A partner? He dreamed of slipping under the sheet with the same person every night, of waking up with that person each morning. Someone he could love. Someone who would love him in return. What a blissful thought.

He came around to the Rue Sainte-Croix-de-la-Bretonnerie and the Rue du Temple. He loved this neighborhood; it was one of Paris's prettiest and trendiest areas. And the nightclubs were wonderful.

The bouncers at his favorite club—two magnificent specimens of testosterone, one black and the other white—let him in right away. He gave them a quick kiss, a "hey there," and a laugh. Then he was pulled into the supercharged atmosphere of the club. He felt a few glances sweep over him, most likely cast by lovers of fresh meat. A guy brushed against his ass; Clément arched his back and bit his lip in a suggestive pose. He was a mix of innocence and ferocity, a male in rut. His eyes paused on the bare torso of a server. It was going to be a good night.

23

The atmosphere in the Parc de la Villette had changed since the discovery of Mathieu Leroy's body. Armed security guards patrolled the area day and night. Several had trained dogs ready to alert their masters to any suspicious activity. Many Parisians were staying away. On the other hand, the park seemed to be drawing more rowdy teenagers, who swore they weren't afraid of anything, especially not the Butcher of Paris. If they saw him, they'd take him down, and if he happened to be gay, so much the better. "We'll kill the fag," they bragged. "He'll be our bitch."

Clément wanted to shout for help. But only a few barely audible groans escaped from his mouth. He was bleeding to death. The pain was unbearable. He thought of his mother. She had always been there for him. He loved her so much. He didn't want to die. He didn't want to cause her grief. Why him? Another groan. He pressed his hands against his stomach as hard as he could. All this blood. His hands were sticky. He felt tears running down his face. He was afraid. Afraid to close his eyes because he knew he'd never open them again. But he was so tired. He was losing hold. It had to stop.

"Hey, there's somebody on the ground over there." The voice was faint, but he heard it. Then footsteps and a cold nose sniffing him. A dog?

"Shit, he's bleeding to death!"

Someone was turning him on his back. But his body felt so numb.

"He's got a pulse! Call an ambulance!"

"Look at his shoulder. He's like the others!"

"Sir, sir, can you hear me?"

He groaned.

"Hang in there. We're getting help."

"Call La Crim' right away. Go do it!"

And then the cold and the dark. Death.

Nico was deep asleep, his face buried in Caroline's neck, his arm across her stomach, his hand on her breast.

His Freddie Mercury ringtone woke him up with a start. It was intruding on their sleep all too often these nights. Caroline purred. She felt wonderful. But Nico knew he had to turn over and answer the phone.

"It's Charlotte, sir. There's been a third attack. He didn't wait long to strike again."

Nico sat up.

"Shit! Same MO?"

"Except for one thing. The victim's on the operating table."

"So he might live?"

"It's touch-and-go. The doctors don't want to say for sure."

"Who is he?"

"Clément Roux. He's twenty-three years old, a chef at the Carré des Feuillants restaurant. Two security guards heard him groaning and found him in one of the architectural follies."

"Which one?" Nico asked. He was now familiar with each of Bernard Tschumi's playful pavilions.

"Le Belvédère," Charlotte replied. "At the southern end of the Prairie du Cercle. My team's there already."

That particular folly offered a bird's-eye view of the park and Claes Oldenberg's monumental sculpture, *Buried Bicycle*, a huge bike saddle, wheel, and handlebars.

"Did he have a shoulder wound?"

"Yes, just like the others."

"We need to sweep the scene before any evidence disappears. And if Clément Roux survives, I want him under protection. The killer failed and might try to finish the job."

"Got it, Chief."

"Has his family been told?"

"His parents are at the hospital. I'll ask them a few questions later."

"Good, but don't wait too long," Nico said.

So the Butcher of Paris had struck again. But he had made a mistake. He hadn't managed to kill his prey. Nico felt sure that his emotional state was worsening, and he was losing control. Beneath his veneer, he had to be a vulnerable person with memories and nightmares. The butcher was now a wounded animal, and the police were tracking him. Still, he was a threat, and he had to be stopped before he attacked yet another young man.

Or maybe exhaustion was setting in, displacing his anger. Were these murders forcing him to confront the void left by his lovers? The same way he had been forced to face the void thirty years ago?

"You've got your work cut out for you, and you could wind up falling on your ass," Michel Cohen had warned him. But Nico's gut told him that he was on the right track.

Who was Damien Forest? Why had Jean-Baptiste told his father that he was a Reuters photographer?

Could this man be a suspect? It was time to answer those questions.

In a few hours, the full excavation of the banquet would begin. Nico prayed that no more surprises would complicate the investigation.

24

"It's urgent," Dr. Xavier Jondeau said over the phone. He was calling Caroline Dalry from the hospital, where Anya had taken a turn for the worse. "We need to make a decision now."

"How soon?" Caroline asked.

"Tomorrow at the very latest."

"Understood. I'll let him know."

It had been a week since the discovery of Jean-Baptiste Cassian's skeleton. His landscape painter friend, Laurent Mercier, had been summoned once more, this time to Magistrate Becker's office.

He was fifty-two—the same age Jean-Baptiste would have been, had he lived. But Jean-Marie Rost thought he looked like an aging adolescent. And not just that. As far as Rost was concerned, he had the mannerisms of a dilettante.

"How long have you been in Vincennes, Mr. Mercier?" Becker asked.

"About ten years now, and we're very happy there." His voice was high-pitched, almost annoyingly so. "You've been married for twenty-seven years," Becker said. "And you had three children with Camille Frot."

"That's right."

Mercier was extraordinarily calm. He had a polite smile on his finely chiseled face. A nice ass and a nicer face, Rost's wife would have observed.

"What was your relationship with Jean-Baptiste Cassian, Mr. Mercier?" Becker asked.

"Um, we were friends, of course."

The two stared at each other. Mercier offered up air-tight alibis for the evenings of the murders. Rost sat and waited. Becker gave him a quick glance. It was time for him to jump in and ask a few questions. But Rost was useless. He had been up with the baby all night, and he had a splitting headache. His only thought was when he'd be able to take two ibuprofens.

"Very well," Becker said. "I must ask you not to leave Paris until we've completed our investigation."

"But of course," said Laurent Mercier.

"Deputy Chief Rost? Are we finished here?"

Rost knew Becker was irritated with him. There was nothing to be done about it. He had a massive headache, and the urgency of the investigation was only adding to it. Hell, between the investigation and the worrying about Nico, everyone at La Crim' was stressed. It didn't help that they had to hide their concern, because show-ing it would have made things even harder for the boss.

"You were one of Jean-Baptiste's best buddies, and you want us to believe that you didn't know who he was sleeping with?" Rost finally said in a quiet voice.

Rost watched as the magistrate's face turned red with anger. He had dropped the ball, and he knew it.

Nico parked at the Place des États-Unis, in front of the Baccarat Museum, with its red panels above the windows and doors. There were some fine pieces in this place: the czar's grand candelabra, glass sets, vases, jewelry… All reminders of his heritage.

Nico crossed the Square Thomas-Jefferson under the chestnut trees' chilly shade. Mothers and children were playing. Farther off, Lafayette and Washington were shaking bronze-cast hands, unaware of everything around them. The square had an American look to it. The benches, streetlamps, and railings were inspired by Battery Park in New York.

Across the street were the Pernod-Ricard headquarters. This was the aniseed empire. In the world of spirits, though, Absolut Vodka had the upper hand. It was an outrage, as far as Anya was concerned, that Absolut was produced in southern Sweden. The country of ABBA had nothing on Russia.

He walked to the end of the square and paused at the monument honoring the fallen Americans who had volunteered to fight for France during World War I. Then he turned onto the Rue Dumont-d'Urville, where he pushed a narrow wrought-iron door open, climbed the stairs to the third floor, and rang Lara Krall Weissman's doorbell.

She was sitting on a white leather couch in a minimalist room. On the wall, a Kandinsky painting caught his attention with its burst of colors. It was a masterpiece.

"What can I do for you?" she asked.

She looked unhappy. The past few days had clearly taken a toll on her.

"Does the name Damien Forest ring a bell?"

"Not at all, no. Should it?"

"Damien Forest was a photographer Jean-Baptiste hired to cover the *tableau-piège*'s burial."

"I wasn't really involved in planning that event. That was all Jean-Baptiste and his father."

Nico sensed some anger in her voice.

"He was a photographer from Reuters," Nico pressed.

"It's a reputable agency. I don't see why that would be a problem."

"The problem is that Damien Forest never worked for Reuters. How could Jean-Baptiste have hired an impostor for such an important event?"

Lara Krall's eyes were twitching.

"We've made a police sketch," Nico said. "I'm going to show it to you. Maybe it'll remind you of someone."

She nodded, but she was looking even more nervous. Exactly what was she afraid of?

Captain Franck Plassard greeted yet another guest from the banquet. He had put in more hours than he could count, but he intended to stay sharp and professional to the finish. He would not allow exhaustion to win out. With each new person, he went back into the ring with the same determination to find a lead that would move the investigation forward.

On the other side of the room, an old gentleman collapsed into a chair and waited patiently for the questions. The man was the retired director of one of France's largest museums. He was a bit deaf, so Plassard had to shout.

"A photographer? Sure, yes, there was one. A young fellow about my daughter's age. That was a long time ago, of course," he said with a wink. He still had a twinkle in his eye. "That reminds me. There's something that happened."

"Yes?" Plassard asked.

"I overheard the photographer and Jean-Baptiste arguing."

"Are you sure of that?"

"As sure as I'm alive."

"Did anyone else hear the argument?"

"No. Maybe you didn't know this, but the Géode was scheduled to be unveiled about two weeks after the banquet-performance. I was fascinated with the way the clouds were reflected on the stainless steel. I left the banquet for a few minutes to go up to the dome. I just wanted to touch it. And I happened upon Jean-Baptiste and the photographer shouting at each other."

Jérôme Dufour from Lyon was sporting a bow tie. Conservative to the core, Deputy Chief Rost thought.

He was nothing like Mercier, with his jeans and pointy-toed shoes, or Vion, with his sartorial allusion to David Beckham. Three men, three styles, and somehow three friends.

"Here's a police sketch of Damien Forest," Magistrate Becker said. "Does he look familiar?"

"No, I'm afraid not."

"Look carefully, Mr. Dufour."

"I'm sorry, but I don't recognize this person."

"Daniel Vion says that you told him Jean-Baptiste Cassian had perhaps gone to the United States. Is that right?"

"Jean-Baptiste's mother was the one who told everyone that."

"Did you hear her say it?"

"No, I didn't. I didn't know his parents very well. Laurent Mercier told me. He talked to the parents every so often."

"And did you believe him?" Becker asked.

"It was better than believing he died in some accident. I preferred to think he was living a quiet life in another country."

"But why would he do that?" Jean-Marie Rost broke in, determined to make amends for his sorry performance during the earlier interview and be an active participant in this one. "Did he think that he had to go to another country to come out of the closet? Here, in France, he was about to marry Lara Krall and start a family. Was he afraid that if he stayed in France he would be forced to live a lie?"

"You're tarnishing his memory!"

"Because I said he was lying and pretending to be someone he wasn't? Or because I said he was gay?"

"Where are you getting this from?"

"Does homosexuality bother you, Mr. Dufour? Scare you, maybe?"

"My God…"

"God loves everybody, Mr. Dufour. Don't you believe that?"

It was Becker's turn to be quiet. Rost couldn't miss the stunned look on his face.

"We need to know where you were and what you were doing last week and last night," Rost said.

"Why?" Dufour asked.

"Did you have sexual relations with Jean-Baptiste Cassian, Mr. Dufour?" Rost shot back.

"I don't know what they were fighting about," the old man said. "But I heard Jean-Baptiste say, 'Don't ask me ever again!'"

"What do you think he was referring to?"

"I have no idea. I'm sorry." The interview room was silent. Plassard finally had his finger on something. But on what, exactly? There had been an altercation between Jean-Baptiste and the photographer. Was it a lovers' quarrel? And had this person decided to take revenge? At this point, there was no way to know.

"What did you say his name was—Damien?" the old man asked suddenly.

"Damien Forest."

"That's not the name Jean-Baptiste used."

"What name did he use?" Plassard said.

"He said, 'Don't ask me ever again, Tim!'"

Lara Krall examined every detail of the composite sketch. Nico was puzzled.

"Does he remind you of someone?"

She shook her head. He couldn't tell if she was upset or relieved.

His phone buzzed in his pocket.

He read the text message from Kriven: "Damien Forest is someone named Tim. Tim and JB had a fight on the sidelines. JB said, 'Don't ask me ever again, Tim!'"

Nico turned this information over in his head and met Lara Krall's eyes.

"I have some news that might help us in our investigation."

She sat up in her chair.

"Your fiancé hired a photographer for the banquet and gave him an assumed name. We need to figure out who this man was and what kind of relationship he had with Jean-Baptiste."

"But I don't recognize this sketch."

"What about a man named Tim? Does that name mean anything to you?"

She didn't say anything, but Nico could tell this piece of information was a blow. He could see it written on her face.

"Absolutely nothing," she said.

Lara Krall was hiding something.

"Very well. I won't take up any more of your time. Don't hesitate to call me if you remember something."

"I'll show you out."

Nico walked back to his car. As he started driving away from the Place des États-Unis, he noticed that Jean-Baptiste Cassian's ex-fiancée was peering at him from an upstairs window. He called Kriven. The commander picked up on the first ring.

"I think we've hit the bull's-eye," Nico said. "Lara Krall is distraught. She knows something about Damien Forest. But she's not talking. Go through her file with a fine-tooth comb. I bet there's a Tim in her group of friends. She'll tell him about my visit. Get someone out here right away to keep an eye on what she does."

"I'm on it."

They were on the right track, he was sure. A moment after he ended the call, his cell phone rang. Kriven, so soon? No, it was Caroline.

"How are you, my love?" he asked with a smile.

"Listen, Nico. I've just finished talking with Dr. Jondeau. Your mother's heart problems are serious. Her ventricular fibrillations are pushing her heart rate to more than six hundred beats per minute. This is very dangerous."

Nico squeezed the steering wheel so hard, his knuckles turned white.

"When there's ventricular fibrillation, and a patient has already had a heart attack, an ICD is recommended."

"What's that?" he asked. He felt a chill running through his veins.

"It's an implantable cardioverter defibrillator, a small device with a powerful battery that weighs hardly more than a couple of ounces. It monitors the heart rhythm. The surgeon embeds the device under the collarbone and attaches electrodes from the device to the heart. If the device detects an irregular heart rhythm, it uses a low-energy electrical pulse to restore the normal rhythm. The device can deliver a high-energy pulse if it's needed."

"Is the operation complicated?"

"It takes a few hours under local anesthetic and sedation. She won't be able to move around much for a few weeks after the procedure. But after that, Anya can have a normal life. She'll set off the alarms at the airport, but otherwise there's no inconvenience."

"Does she know?"

"Not yet. Dr. Jondeau asked me to go with him to tell her. Tanya's with her now."

"I'm glad you'll be there. I don't think I can get to the hospital."

"I thought as much. I'm going to be at Bichat Hospital for a meeting anyway. And I think Alexis will be at Bichat too."

"Thank you, sweetheart. When do they want to operate?"

"Tomorrow, if possible."

Nico took a moment to absorb the shock.

"I'll call you in a bit," Caroline said. "They're paging me."

A life-saving foreign body in his full-blooded Russian mother's chest. It would have made him laugh if it weren't so scary.

25

She stayed at the window for a long while without moving. Minutes passed slowly after Chief Sirsky's car disappeared around the corner. Lara Krall felt emptied out and destroyed. Her whole life had been nothing but torture.

Losing Jean-Baptiste ate at her every day; the years hadn't taken the edge off. She was still in love with his gentle grin and his optimism, creativity, and charm. Her dreams had become a nightmare when he vanished. There were so many questions. Why? How? Whose fault was it? She had never made peace with his disappearance. And now she knew that Jean-Baptiste was dead the whole time.

What if he'd done it? If he was the guilty one, she would die too.

26

"Lara Krall has an older brother named Timothy. Isn't that interesting?" Kriven said as Nico walked into his office. "He's a photographer of sorts. He's listed on a few photography websites but doesn't have a site of his own. I found some other tidbits, too."

"And where does he live?"

"He lives at 32 Rue des Vinaigriers in the tenth arrondissement. It's between the Boulevard Magenta and the Quai de Valmy. She headed over there a half hour after you left her place."

"I'll let Becker know right away."

The powers of the French police were spelled out by law and strictly enforced. Like police anywhere else, they could make arrests when someone was caught committing a crime or when there was probable cause. But many other situations required an order from the investigating magistrate. In this case, it was up to Becker to issue an order to take Timothy Krall into custody for questioning. They'd put him in a cell to scare him.

Alexandre Becker drew up the papers, and Nico got everyone moving. With Kriven, Plassard, and Vidal, they drove off in two cars toward the Boulevard du Palais and the Pont-au-Change. They crossed the Place du Châtelet with sirens wailing and lights flashing. On the sidewalks, the crowds turned and stared. Children excitedly pointed at the cars speeding by. The Boulevard de Sébastopol belched thick traffic, as always, but they managed to navigate around the cars. At the Boulevard de Strasbourg, they turned toward the Gare de l'Est to bypass the Rue du Château-d'Eau. The street was usually crowded and so narrow that traffic was often at a standstill. Just ahead, Indian restaurants offered basmati rice and beignets for a few euros. The police cars split up at the Saint-Laurent church. The Boulevard Magenta, nearly a hundred feet across, let them speed up and dive into the Rue des Vinaigriers. There, they finally slowed down; the narrow artery, lined with stores and restaurants, felt like a village. They drove through the Rue Lucien-Sampaix intersection. A drugstore was on one corner, and a bakery and candy store were on the other. They were in the heart of the tenth arrondissement, with its two main train stations, the Canal Saint-Martin, the boulevards, and the neighborhoods that had given birth to the French can-can.

Nico and his men parked by Poursin, which had made copper and brass buckles since 1830, and its old-fashioned window displays. Farther off, number 32 was between the Philippe bookstore and the Santa Sed, a Chilean restaurant with its metal gate still lowered. Nico saw a school desk in the bookstore and thought of how the shop was probably filled with as much treasure as Ali Baba's cave. His eyes met those of a customer seated on a couch. Then he turned toward number 32, its wine-colored door filthy and damaged. The building was in need of a facelift.

"On the fifth floor," Kriven said as he entered the dark hallway.

Plassard bounded ahead, ready to draw his Sig Sauer SP 2022 automatic. Nico climbed the stairs more slowly. The cops would grab Tim any minute now. He'd have to pack a bag and put in a few clothes and toiletries before spending his night elsewhere. Perhaps he would never return to this place. According to Kriven, Lara's brother had dreamed of being a great photographer. But he had failed. He did shoots now and then for overbooked wedding photographers and managed to sell a few prints to pay the rent. But he also needed help from Lara, and Nico surmised that this was the cause of frequent fights with her husband, Gregory Weissman. Weissman considered her brother a loser. He hated him.

The filthy and damaged door on the Rue des Vinaigriers was a far cry from the pomp of the Place des États-Unis and the celebrity of Samuel Cassian's banquet-performance. It was also a far cry from Jean-Baptiste's exhibition in New York.

Tim was hurtling down the stairs. Nico heard the man gasping for air. He had to be searching for a hiding spot.

"David!" Nico shouted.

There was a silhouette, a backpack. Tim seemed to be having a hard time figuring out what to do. Hide or run? A moment later, he made his decision. He dashed outside, with Vidal nipping at his heels.

Nico started running, and the other two men followed. They reached the drugstore and bakery at the corner of the Rue Lucien-Sampaix. Across the street were Le Flash, a convenience store, and the Deux Singes restaurant, which offered a ten-euro *prix-fixe* lunch. Tim seemed to be losing steam and was looking desperate. Finally, they closed in on him. "Police! Stop!" Nico shouted a few feet from the fugitive.

Tim seemed to be deaf. Nico grabbed his shoulder. The suspect tried to extricate himself, but Captain Vidal, who had just caught up, took aim at him.

"Calm down," Nico said.

Clearly afraid and confused, Tim collapsed on the concrete.

"Timothy Krull?" Nico asked.

The man did not reply. His hair was dripping with sweat. There was panic and hate in his eyes. Kriven grabbed his arms, and Plassard searched his pockets. He took out his wallet and found an ID card.

"Timothy Krall," he confirmed. "Thirty-one Rue des Vinaigriers, 75010 Paris. It's him."

"Timothy Krall, we're taking you into custody," Nico said.

He was this much closer to keeping his promise. But would it be close enough to save his mother?

27

Police could keep someone in custody for twenty-four hours without pressing charges. With a magistrate's authorization, they could extend the period. Suspected terrorists or members of organized crime rings could be jailed for as long as six days before facing any charges.

They used their limited time to overwhelm Tim, undermine him, and force a confession. Nico called in colleagues to help with what they called a *bertillonage*, a technique they sometimes used when they wanted to make a suspect miserable. It was named after Alphonse Bertillon, who in 1891 devised a biometric method of identification that involved taking the dimensions and identifying characteristics of a suspect. In Bertillon's day, measurements included height and reach, as well as width of head, size of ears, and length of the feet. The method was flawed, however, and using fingerprints as a means of identification soon succeeded the Bertillon method.

Now, the term *bertillonage* referred to strategic use of procedure. The officers took mug shots and fingerprints. They also took a DNA swab from inside his cheek. He was free to refuse, but that was an offense publishable by a year in prison or a fifteen-thousand-euro fine. They shuffled him back and forth many times between the cell and the cops' offices, where he was treated like the worst criminal.

The holding cells were Spartan at best. The floor area of each was barely a few square feet. There was no ventilation, and a bench was the sole piece of furniture. Vidal and Almeida brought Tim a mattress for the night, which he had to squeeze between a wall and an unbreakable glass window. The view was depressing: an imposing guard sitting in a chair. No hope of escape. Timothy Krall, the fifty-year-old failed photographer, was scared to death. That was Nico's intention. Officers came in to handcuff him again and take him to an interrogation room.

"All yours," Nico said to Becker.

An investigating magistrate was expected to use any legal means necessary to get at the truth, and that didn't necessarily mean telling the truth. It was up to Becker to decide if the evidence was sufficient to send the suspect in front of a court, which was the only way to determine his culpability. The French judicial system was founded on the presumption of innocence, so Nico wanted a detailed and signed confession that would hold up. The door closed, and Becker sat across from the suspect. Tim looked like a mouse caught in a trap.

"I'll get right to the point, Mr. Krall," Becker said. "Do you admit taking the false identity of Damien Forest, a Reuters photographer, in order to cover Samuel Cassian's banquet-performance thirty years ago in the Parc de la Villette?"

Tim licked his dry lips.

"Yes," he replied hoarsely.

"Was Samuel Cassian aware of your true identity?"

"No."

"To your knowledge, did he have any reason to believe that you were Lara Krall's brother?"

"No, I don't think so. No."

"Did you know Jean-Baptiste Cassian, your sister's fiancé?"

"Yes, of course."

"Was Jean-Baptiste Cassian informed of your presence at the banquet-performance?"

"Yes!"

Becker registered the tension in Timothy Krall's face.

"What was your reason for pretending to be Damien Forest?"

"They needed a professional photographer."

"And you weren't one?"

"I was unemployed."

"Did Jean-Baptiste Cassian agree to lie for you?"

"He wanted to help me. I was broke. I needed the money."

"A witness caught you arguing with him that day. What was the argument about?"

Tim's eyes widened. He looked stupefied.

"A witness?" he asked. Becker could see that he was trying to recall the scene. Then his body sagged.

"Jean-Baptiste had already helped me several times. He said he'd had enough."

"He said..." Alexandre Becker leaned over the thick folder on the desk and leafed through the pages one by one, raising the tension in the room. "'Don't ask me ever again, Tim!'" he read out loud. "What had you been asking him, Mr. Krall?"

"I'd asked him for help with work. That's all."

"And what, specifically, was Jean-Baptiste referring to?"

"Lying to his father for me, I suppose."

"You *suppose*?"

"Yes... I don't know!"

Becker spread the photos of Jean Baptiste on the table. "Did you take these photos, Mr. Krall?"

"No."

"Who could have taken them?"

"I don't know! And that's the least of my worries."

"Jean-Baptiste Cassian was found dead, Mr. Krall. Killed thirty years ago, shortly after the *tableau-piège*'s burial."

"I had nothing to do with that! I didn't kill him if that's what you're thinking!"

Lara Krall had been taken into another interrogation room under the eaves. The heat was stifling. It wasn't a trick. The air-conditioning was broken.

Nico put on his poker face and sat down opposite her. She had lied to him, and they both knew it.

"Mrs. Weissman, it's clear that your brother, Timothy Krall, pretended to be Damien Forest, a Reuters photographer, at Samuel Cassian's banquet thirty years ago. Were you aware of this?"

Lara Krall's years were hanging on her like dead weight.

"Yes," she said.

"How did you learn this?"

"Tim told me."

"Were you aware that Samuel Cassian, your future father-in-law, and his guests were taken advantage of?"

Her lips were trembling now.

"I… I never saw it that way."

But of course not.

"Tim was having financial difficulties. Jean-Baptiste was willing to help him. And my brother was a good photographer. I didn't see the harm."

"Evidently, your brother's financial situation hasn't changed. I imagine you still help him regularly?"

She looked down. Nico could tell she was confused. Tim was probably Jean-Baptiste's complete opposite.

"That wasn't a small thing that Jean-Baptiste did for your brother. He was willing to lie to his father. And what if the photos hadn't turned out? It would have been a disaster. This wasn't just a banquet, after all. It was an art event designed to span three decades. Jean-Baptiste was willing to go out on quite a limb for your brother."

"Jean-Baptiste wasn't taking any risk as far as my brother's abilities were concerned."

Tears had started to stream down her cheeks. Nico sensed that the woman had died on a June night thirty years ago, when her fiancé disappeared. Since then, she had walked through life as though it were an immense, dry, and dangerous desert.

"During the banquet, a witness overheard an altercation between Jean-Baptiste and your brother. Did they have any reason to fight?"

"Timothy could be tiresome. He always seemed to think that we owed him, as if making him happy and successful was our responsibility. I suppose Jean-Baptiste had had enough. He was right; I wouldn't have reproached him for it."

"Your fiancé told him, 'Don't ask me ever again, Tim!' What was he referring to?"

"He was probably sick of putting up with Tim."

There was a knock on the door, and a guard gave Nico a note from Deputy Chief Rost: "Gregory has just arrived in the building."

"Their argument could have escalated, and your brother could have killed Jean-Baptiste out of rage or jealousy," Nico suggested.

"My brother didn't kill Jean-Baptiste!" Lara Krall shouted. "That's impossible! He'd never do that to me!"

"Was Tim aware of your fiancé's infidelity?"

Lara's rapid blinking told Nico that she was petrified. "Yes," she said.

"How did he find out?"

"I felt horrible. I had to tell someone."

"And you picked Tim, your brother."

Lara had taken the wrong person into her confidence. Nico surmised that Lara's immature and unstable brother had taken advantage of the information.

"Did you specify the nature, back then, of this relationship? Let me be clear: Did you tell Tim that Jean-Baptiste had been involved with another man?

Lara Krall's face flushed. Tim knew Jean-Baptiste's secret.

"I'd like to know how Jean-Baptiste Cassian agreed to give you the job of photographing the banquet-performance, Mr. Krall," Becker said. "He was lying to his father and risked being found out."

"My photos were good! And nobody else would give me a chance."

"That's not what I'm asking, Mr. Krall. Much had to be at stake for Jean-Baptiste Cassian to lie for you. The burial of his father's final *tableau-piège* was a major event. Samuel wanted to avoid even the smallest mistake."

"Let's say he owed me."

"Okay, he owed you," Becker said. He was getting angry. "What was it, exactly, that he owed you?"

"Let's just keep it at that," Krall said.

Alexandre Becker suspected that this man had all the qualities of a blackmailer.

"I think Jean-Baptiste was buying your silence."

Tim stood up.

"Your sister is being interrogated, Mr. Krall," Becker said. He closed in on the failed photographer. Becker wanted him to think that Lara Krall was telling the police everything. There was no point in trying to weasel out. "Did you know that Jean-Baptiste was cheating on your sister?"

"Yes, Lara confided in me," he finally said.

"With a man."

He shrugged.

"You had information that could have hurt Jean-Baptiste, and you used it to get the job of photographing the banquet-performance, didn't you?"

"It's true, okay! I threatened to out him to his family. I had him by the short hairs."

"Jean-Baptiste lost his temper," Becker said. "He wanted to put an end to your game, even if it meant that his secret was disclosed. That would have been the end for you. Everybody would have known what you were: a dirtbag, scum who'd throw anyone under the bus. So you killed him."

"No! I didn't touch the arrogant little faggot! I was in control. He was afraid of me!"

Becker didn't speak. He was a dirtbag, yes. But that didn't mean he was a murderer.

"Did Tim threaten Jean-Baptiste? Did he tell Jean-Baptiste that he'd out him if he wasn't hired to photograph the *tableau-piège*?"

"Jean-Baptiste would never have lied to his father if he hadn't been cornered. But why would my brother have killed Jean-Baptiste? There was nothing in it for him."

Lara Krall had clearly thought things over.

"Maybe things got out of hand. Jean-Baptiste could have told your brother that he wouldn't be blackmailed any longer, even if it meant coming out. Maybe your brother lost control."

Nico was no longer talking in terms of a one-night stand, which was what Jean-Baptiste had confessed to Lara. He had used the words "coming out." Lara didn't dispute them.

"My brother couldn't have killed Jean-Baptiste. It's impossible," she said.

"Are you sure about that?"

Leaving the interrogation room, Nico walked past Gregory Weissman, who looked exactly as he'd envisioned. Being dragged to police headquarters because of his wife clearly had him fuming. Poor Lara, who had refused to be happy since Jean-Baptiste's disappearance and had opted for a marriage of convenience—which had become an interminable prison sentence. And all this time, the idea that her brother could have played a role in this drama had been tearing her apart.

He went back to his office and his team members, who were waiting for him. Despite the late hour, they were all gathered around his desk. Nico could see the fatigue on their faces. Becker joined them and took a seat.

"Timothy has the guiltiest face I've ever seen and a motive, too," he said.

"We don't have any concrete proof," Nico countered.

"All we have to do is get him to admit when and how he killed his future brother-in-law, and we'll be done," Becker said.

"Let's check his alibis for the nights of the Villette attacks."

"What if Jean-Baptiste's murder and the attacks in the park are unrelated, Nico?"

"I don't think so," he said. He was also tired, and his voice betrayed his irritation.

Claire Le Marec cleared her throat to diffuse the tension.

"What does Krall do with his free time?" Nico asked more calmly. "I think he has plenty of it."

"He has been unable to maintain a relationship with a woman for more than a few months," Becker said. "They all left him. He sounds like a complete homophobe. He called Jean-Baptiste an 'arrogant little faggot.' But I still can't see him all that motivated to attack young men in a park."

"We've got some time left to keep questioning him and get a clearer idea of his involvement."

"Nico, if we don't have anything more by tomorrow evening, I'll have to release him."

"Give me the benefit of the doubt, Alexandre. Tim might be the attacker and just playing dumb with us."

"You still think there's just one perpetrator. Okay." Becker sighed. "Commander Maurin can examine his alibis carefully. If something turns up, I'll extend his stay with us."

"Thank you, Alexandre. What would you say if Rost and Kriven took over the questioning?"

"I won't decline the offer. You know how to reach me if you need to."

Nico smiled at his friend, the magistrate.

"Charlotte, are there any other suspects?" he asked.

"The night of the attacks, Nathan Sellière, the antiquarian, was at home. He says he was alone, so we have nobody to confirm this. That said, he doesn't match up with the murderer's profile. And he had an exhibition at his gallery on Wednesday night. He closed the gallery at around one in the morning. The room Florian Bonnet was found in was paid for at twelve thirty in the morning. So the timing is off."

"So we can cross Dufour and Sellière off our list," Nico said.

"That leaves Laurent Mercier and Daniel Vion. Mercier had a dinner with clients Tuesday night in Paris."

"Did his wife confirm that?" Becker asked.

"Yes. I contacted those clients and the Hôtel du Louvre, where they met. Specifically Le Defender, the bar there. It's a cozy place with Second-Empire-style curtains. Lots of cocktails, and it's open until one thirty in the morning."

"What time did he get back home?" Nico asked.

"At midnight, according to his wife. But I get the feeling that she's the type to do what her husband says, and she'd protect him any way she could."

"What about Vion?"

"Daniel Vion wasn't able to give us a clear alibi. He's still in the running."

"So we have two suspects," Becker said. "Assuming that Jean-Baptiste's murderer is the attacker in the park."

"Two, plus Timothy Krall. Everybody's going to be questioned again. What do you think of these suspects?" Nico asked Becker and Rost.

"You and David interviewed Daniel Vion first, so you have a handle on him," Jean-Marie Rost replied. "Despite being close to Jean-Baptiste, he had no suspicions that he was gay."

"But Sophie Bayle wasn't surprised, which means Daniel Vion is completely clueless, or he's lying," Kriven said.

"And Mercier?"

"Our deputy chief has some candid views on him," Becker said, giving Rost a wink.

"He's a pretty boy," Rost said. "A fifty-two-year-old who's trying to pass for thirty. It's pathetic. To his credit, Mercier knew that something was off with Jean-Baptiste. He didn't play naïve the way Daniel Vion did, although he apparently didn't know about any problems Jean-Baptiste and Lara were having. He ended up marrying Camille and lives with her and their three children. Happily ever after. He didn't recognize any of the portraits. And unlike Daniel Vion, Laurent Mercier has an alibi for the attack on Tuesday night. Charlotte will have to verify it. I'll wrap all this up with a side thought. Dufour told Vion that Jean-Baptiste fled to the United States. Dufour heard it from Mercier. Mercier got it firsthand from Jean-Baptiste's mother. Quite a game of telephone."

"What about Plassard and company? Where are they in their interviews?" Nico asked.

"They're coming to the end of their list," Kriven replied. "They're not letting up. They got that one juicy tidbit, and you never know if something else might crop up."

Nico smiled. Plassard had uncovered the gem about Timothy Krall's argument with Jean-Baptiste.

"The excavation's under way," Becker said. "They're going slowly to ensure that they don't disturb the scientific and artistic aspects of the project."

"It's going to be a few days before they know whether Cassian's skeleton has any companions," Deputy Chief Rost said.

"Well, one thing's for sure. That lunch in the park was no picnic for Jean-Baptiste Cassian," Kriven said.

"No, it wasn't. It's going to be a long night if we expect to get to the bottom of this," the chief said.

"Don't forget, we can't hold Timothy Krall forever," Alexandre Becker warned.

Maurin's phone rang.

"My crime scene investigator," she said as she looked at the screen and hit speakerphone.

Authorized by Becker, the investigator had gone to the hospital to examine the still-unconscious Clément Roux—the man attacked in the architectural folly and found alive, by some miracle.

"I'm done here," the investigator told Maurin. "The shape and depth of the cut were identical to those found on the other victims. But there's something else. A bit of ultraviolet ink on the back of the victim's hand. It's a stamp from a club—invisible except under a black light."

"And legible?" Charlotte asked.

"He got it last night. I have the name of the place; it's in the Marais. I'll text you the location."

"Good job."

"Do you think Clément Roux met his attacker there?"

"It's a definite possibility."

"His parents haven't left the hospital, and the men haven't been able to talk with them at length. Clément Roux is gay, which his mother has known for a long time. His father's had more trouble accepting it, but he's there and just as upset as his wife."

"Is their son going to make it?"

"Not sure yet. All right, I'm coming back to headquarters. I'm guessing we're spending the night and possibly longer."

They ended the call.

"We'll have to go to the club tonight, with a photo of Clément Roux and recent ones of Timothy Krall, Laurent Mercier, and Daniel Vion. Let's not forget that synthetic hairs were found on the first victim, Mathieu Leroy. The attacker probably altered his looks to avoid being recognized."

The room went quiet.

"I'll go," Nico said, breaking the silence.

As the chief of the Criminal Investigation Division, Nico could participate in an investigation in any way that he wanted. His officers admired Nico for being a fully involved leader instead someone who sat behind his desk and accepted medals without dirtying his hands.

"Women aren't allowed in that bar," Maurin said.

"All right, then I'll take Ayoub Moumen with me."

Nobody would be sitting around tonight. His mother's operation was scheduled for the morning, so he had to make the most of the time he had.

28

Two hulking bouncers stood at the entrance. They barely blinked as they waved regulars through and gave newcomers a once-over. Moumen held his badge up, and the man nodded. The captain had led an investigation there recently and knew the place well. Nico let him take the lead.

"You're new here," the bouncer told Nico as he eyed him greedily.

"He's with me," Moumen interjected.

"Normally I'd have to search him."

Nico felt like he was being undressed.

"Come on, John!" Moumen said, taking the bouncer by the arm and whispering in his ear. "We're here on official business. Just let us do our jobs."

The bouncer stepped aside, and the two officers entered the club. The deafening music pierced Nico's ears and thudded against his chest. The shadowy vestibule looked like a train platform where anonymous travelers merged. Once again, Nico felt eyes on him.

They paid the cover charge and got an ultraviolet stamp. Nico followed Moumen into a cramped hallway with a lit floor. Patrons hurried through the passageway to the dance floor. The strobe lights blinded Nico for a few moments. Adjusting his eyes, he made out the disco balls and the glittery specks of light they were throwing on the ceiling and walls. Speakers were belching out music: "Fancy Footwork," an electrofunk hit by Chromeo. The energized crowd yelled out the duo's suggestive lyrics.

The men wriggled and ground against each other, a sweaty sheen on their bare torsos.

Moumen led them to the bar, where they sat down on chrome stools. Nico marveled at how this man could blend in. He certainly had the looks. Seductive deep-brown eyes, long eyelashes, an easy smile, honey-colored skin. He wasn't above flirting, but everyone at headquarters knew he was devoted to his wife, the mother of his children.

"Can I get you something?" Moumen yelled above the music.

"A soda."

"What did you say?"

Nico tried again. "A soda!"

"You think they have that here?" Moumen shouted back. "I was toying with the idea of getting you drunk and taking advantage of your athletic body. Just my luck. You know, there are some really nice rooms underground. You'd love them."

"Maybe another time. But sorry, it wouldn't be with you."

"You just broke my heart."

The bartender appeared, interrupting their banter.

"Can we have two cranberry vodkas, please," Moumen said.

"Coming right away, my prince," he responded.

"Vodka, cranberry juice, orange liqueur, and pineapple liqueur," Moumen warned.

Nico didn't know if it would agree with him. He had just gotten over a stomach ulcer.

"The bartender's name is Enzo. He's a handsome beast. So much the better for customers."

Moumen set the picture of Clément Roux on the bar.

"Do you recognize this man?" he asked Enzo, who had just returned with their drinks.

"Clément? Sure, he's a regular. A sweet guy."

"Did you see him last night?"

"He was dancing with an older guy." Enzo slipped over to another customer.

Adam Lambert, the glam-rock star, was bawling out "What Do You Want From Me." On the dance floor, the bodies were melding together.

"Enzo!" Moumen yelled. "Come back here."

Enzo returned, a phony smile on his face.

"Enzo, Nico. Nico, Enzo. Oh, that rhymes! You'll get along great."

"And what can I do for you, Nico?" the bartender asked. He held a finger to his lips as the crowd started singing along with pop vocalist Jenifer.

Nico waited for the song to end. Then he pressed on. "Clément was attacked. We're looking for the man he left with."

"What? Attacked? Shit! How is he?"

"It's still touch and go. I want to show you some pictures. Can you tell me if you recognize the man who was with Clément?"

"Okay, I'll look at the pictures, but only if you buy me a drink."

The crowd started singing again.

Nico held the pictures of the three suspects out to Enzo.

"No, not him. Clément wouldn't have been attracted to this guy."

He was pointing to Timothy Krall.

"The others are entirely possible, but I'm not sure. Clément and his buddy went downstairs pretty fast. You should talk to the DJ down there. He's Clément's friend."

"Thanks, Enzo."

"No problem. Come back anytime. You're always welcome here."

"You've got a magic touch," Moumen said lightly as they stepped off the stools. "Shall we go downstairs?"

They made their way down a hall packed with vampires ready to sink their teeth into innocent necks. They came to a back room, which seemed gigantic in comparison. A flashy bar spilled bluish light over the room, including the corners, where kissing and fondling couples lay on couches. Nico couldn't help feeling uncomfortable as he watched the lovers explore their partners' muscled chests with their hands and their half-open lips with their tongues.

Several eyes locked on Nico. He felt them looking him over. His six-foot-three-inch frame, blond hair, and clear blue eyes seemed to be up for grabs. But surely the men also sensed that he was the kind of guy who took charge.

Gaëtan Roussel came on. Men got off the couches and started dancing. They belted out his lyrics:

"Inside outside
Sinbad is coming back
Don't leave me, my baby
Don't, on his way back."

One of the men winked. Nico smiled politely and turned away.

Moumen led him to the DJ at the end of the room. The go-go dancers were lathering themselves under the ceiling-mounted showers. By the DJ's corner there were labyrinthine hallways, passageways that plunged into absolute darkness. Men ambled in. Their aim was straightforward: to trade erotic pleasures in anonymity. They aroused themselves and each other in private rooms with porn. Nico was overwhelmed by the smell of semen. But at this late hour, what else could he expect?

"Hey there, Ayoub!" the DJ said. "You've got someone with you."

"He's my boss."

"Hi, boss!"

A smooth, feminine voice came on.

"That's Lilly Wood and the Prick, a French pop group that sings in English," the DJ told them. "There's some Johnny Cash and Patti Smith in the lyrics. I think you'll like it, Mr. Boss. They're awesome."

"We came about Clément," Moumen said directly.

"Is something wrong?"

"Someone made a bloody mess of him last night."

"Clément? That can't be."

"He's in the hospital. He's not out of the woods. We think he met his attacker here. Do you remember who he was with?"

"I'd never seen the man before. Average height, sorta skinny, and clean. He looked pretentious. But I'll tell you this: Clément was hooked, and he was set on spending the night with him."

Nico handed him the picture of Tim Krall.

"Not our kind of guy. Too sloppy."

"And what about these guys?"

The DJ shrugged.

"Take another look for my boss," Moumen said.

"Oh, your boss! He's not a hard one to look at." The DJ laughed as he leaned on Moumen's shoulder. "You like alternative rock? The Train from San Francisco? I like their single from Christmas. Everybody listen up! We're playing this for Clément, our buddy, so he'll come back to us."

He put "Shake Up Christmas" on the turntable and raised the volume. Nico recognized it right away. Coca-Cola had used it in a commercial.

"Clément and his guy were here until late, as usual," the DJ yelled. "Gianni and Théo over there might know more." He gestured toward the dance floor. Nico paused. Gianni and Theo were two of the men who had locked eyes on him a few minutes earlier. They were still watching.

"Should I offer them a drink?" Moumen asked, pretending to be naïve. He was enjoying the situation.

"I'll wait for you here," Nico said curtly.

He watched as the second-in-command from Maurin's group swayed across the dance floor to get the two men. Nico found a couch. He was exhausted. He took out his cell phone and sent Caroline a text. "At a club, a place where you'd never get in. Just want to hug you now. Miss you." Her reply was immediate. Caroline had a hard time sleeping when he was out. "Miss you too. Be careful! Hugs back. And more if you want." He felt warmth spread through him.

"I'm Gianni," one of his admirers said in a deep voice.

Nico doubted that this was his real name. It seemed more like an assumed name for his nighttime activities. Gianni was sitting next to him already. Nico felt the man's thigh pressing against his.

"And I'm Théo," the other man said. This one had turned his attention away from Nico and was now ogling Moumen.

They had both found their special someones.

"I saw you when you came in," Gianni said.

His black fishnet T-shirt showed off his flawless muscles. Nico guessed that Gianni had a matching thong.

"I know," Nico replied.

"Are you free tonight?"

His thigh was pressing even harder against Nico's. And now Gianni's hand was on Nico's thigh. Best to be forthright.

"Not tonight," Nico said with a smile.

"Another time? You're my type."

"You're too kind, but... I'm in a relationship."

"Oh, you're faithful?"

"Indeed."

"That's so refreshing!"

"With a woman," Nico said.

Gianni frowned. "Are you messing with me?"

"Not at all."

"There's no swaying you?" he asked.

Moumen was trying to extricate himself from Théo, who had managed to plant a kiss on his cheek. Gianni, at least, had shown some restraint.

"No, I'm in love with her."

"I hope she's worth it."

"She absolutely is."

"Even in bed?"

Despite the dark passageways and rooms, there was no privacy in this place. Nico realized how easy it would be to pick someone up. The target of a predator, Clément hadn't stood a chance.

"Yes, no one could be better," Nico said with a sly smile.

"What are you doing here, then? Are you a cop like Ayoub?"

"Chief of the Criminal Investigative Division, in fact. It's a pleasure to meet you." Nico held out his hand.

Gianni shook it. "I'm a lawyer. I travel between Paris and New York. Coming here is my way of relaxing. My straight colleagues cheat on their wives, and they have no problem with it. They do have a problem with any colleagues who might be gay. But we're working on it. Attitudes are changing."

The DJ started playing Dido's "Here With Me." Nico liked the blend of soul and Celtic influences.

"We're here about Clément. He was attacked after visiting the club last night. Somebody was with him."

Nico took out the picture of Timothy Krall.

"Don't recognize him," Gianni said. He passed the picture to Theo, who also shook his head.

"Tell me about the guy who left with him," Nico said.

"Clément came alone, so they met here," Gianni said.

"And what was your impression?"

"Not my type. He was too skinny. I like men about my size. Like you."

They were shouting into each other's ears; the music was deafening.

"Clément didn't have the same taste in men?"

"He's attracted to mysterious guys. This one nabbed Clément but wouldn't kiss him. That's pretty much how he nailed him. He'd tease and deny. Some guys like that."

"Do any of these photos look familiar?"

Laurent Mercier and Daniel Vion were looking at the camera in the photos Nico showed Gianni.

"This guy had blue eyes. Not as pretty as yours, of course. He was wearing a white and gold crew neck. And he had chestnut hair and a beard. It could have been a disguise. He might have been one of the two men, but don't take me at my word. Sorry I can't be more helpful. I know it's important to you and Clément."

"And you didn't notice anything else that was unusual about the way he was acting?"

"I'm trying to remember. Why don't we dance? I have to think, and sometimes I can do that best when I'm on my feet. Don't worry. It'll be entirely innocent. I'm not an idiot."

Nico was starting to like this man.

"Well?" Gianni said.

"If Ayoub agrees to a dance with Théo, then I'll dance too."

Gianni gave Théo a thumbs-up. Théo smiled and puffed his chest at a plainly stunned Moumen. Nico couldn't help laughing.

"I like your attitude," Gianni said. "There's no harm in sharing a dance."

"Could I ask a question?" Nico said. "You said the man Clément was with was skinny. Could you tell me a little bit more about his looks?"

"Oh sure. Like I said, he was a bit thin for my taste. And the way he moved was too prissy for me. Like a little girl."

"A girl? Anything you can add to that?"

"Hmm, I remember now: he had this tic when he talked. He rubbed his finger over his lower lip the whole time. Not the tip of his finger, but the middle part of his finger, like this…"

He imitated Clément Roux's attacker.

"Well, that's actually a very useful detail," Nico said. "Does anything else come to mind?"

"That's all I have. Shall we dance? Don't worry. I won't rub up against the chief of police."

"Yes, we'll dance."

Gianni's eyes sparkled. But Nico's thoughts were on the Butcher of Paris and that tic, which could reveal who he was, despite any disguise. Better yet: Gianni had said he was like a "little girl." It was valuable information well worth a dance.

29

Daylight had hardly broken when Nico parked his car in the hospital parking lot. After leaving the nightclub with Captain Moumen, he should have gone straight to headquarters, but he knew he would regret it if he didn't see his mother before she went into the operating room.

He ran all the way to his mother's unit. The nurses were going from one bed to the next, their faces serious and their smiles practiced. It made Nico think of flight attendants handling passengers during an engine failure.

"Chief Sirsky?" one of them said.

He had asked Caroline to intercede. Visiting a patient so early in the morning was usually forbidden. But nurses always deferred to doctors, even if they practiced at another hospital.

"Nico, how are you?" Anya murmured when she saw him.

Mothers were all the same, protective of their children, even at the oddest moments.

"I'm well, *Maman*. How are you?"

He sat by the bed and held her hand in his.

"I'm so glad this is going to be over soon, and I will be able to go home. I've had enough of this circus."

"I saw the priest at Saint-Serge," he said quietly.

She smiled indulgently.

"I know, Nico."

He stared at her.

"We Russians are everywhere—even in this hospital. A nurse has been bringing me messages from everybody in the community. And the priest has been here to visit. He hopes that you'll introduce him to Caroline. He'd love to meet her."

"He doesn't know Dimitri, does he? He seemed to imply that he did."

Anya's smile grew wider, and her eyes shone, despite her pallor.

"That's a little secret between Dimitri and me. He's eager to learn our history. You're aware of that. We've been meeting with Father. Oh, I haven't done anything that you might object to. I know that any religious instruction must be your decision. But I hope that someday you'll allow him to attend Mass with me."

She ran out of breath.

"Maybe I'll make a good Orthodox boy out of him! It wouldn't hurt you to attend a few Masses yourself, Nico," she added with a wink. "Considering your job, you could use a little religion."

"Maybe I will, *Maman*." He kissed her on the cheek.

"The procedure will go well. Don't worry."

Nico wasn't quite sure, right then, which of them had said the words.

"I'm sure of it," he said.

30

Nico returned to his office, more nervous than ever. He had asked Caroline to go to the hospital and stay there until Anya woke up. Caroline, as understanding and generous as ever, had agreed. Nico couldn't bear the thought of not being at the hospital when his mother went under the knife. But she would understand. He couldn't do anything for her at the hospital anyway. But he could do everything in his power at headquarters to apprehend Jean-Baptiste Cassian's murderer and the Butcher of Paris. He had to keep his promise and honor his end of the deal.

Nico went up Stairwell A. On the fourth floor, Moumen was leaning against the department's symbol on the wall—a thistle and the motto "Brush against us and you get stung." Nico was every bit as prickly. Nobody would dare to needle him this morning.

"We're all here, Chief," Moumen said, standing at attention.

"Everyone in my office now. Is Becker here?"

"He's on his way."

Moumen was happy. His little trip with the boss had swelled his head.

Nico was already on his way down the narrow corridor to his office. Moumen left to round up his colleagues.

Clare Le Marec brought warm croissants to the meeting; their aroma filled the room. Jean-Marie finished a text to his wife. Kriven and Plassard set their cups of hot coffee on the table. Moumen pulled the chair out for

Commander Maurin, who smiled with a bit of exasperation. Alexandre Becker set a thick folder on the table—the
one about Jean-Baptiste Cassian's murder. Then he pulled
an accordion folder with a strap and metal clasp out of
his briefcase. It had a compartment for each of the recent
victims. Becker was now on top of these cases too, which
meant that Nico's suspicions were being taken seriously.

"You've spent all night at the clubs, so we're eager to
hear what you've turned up. That is, if you're comfortable telling us. It might be too personal," Becker said,
winking at his friend.

"We picked up some juicy stuff, all right," Nico retorted.
"Didn't we, Ayoub?"

"The boss is right." Moumen looked around the table.
"He had to sell his body for a few leads. But they were
high-quality leads."

"Really? Do tell us," Kriven said.

"We met Gianni and Théo, two regulars at the
nightclub Clément Roux usually goes to," Nico said,
getting serious again. "The young man met an older
guy, according to the bartender. And it wasn't Timothy
Krall. On that point everyone agreed. According them,
Clément Roux would have never been attracted to a guy
like Tim."

Maurin raised her hand.

"Timothy Krall has an airtight alibi for Wednesday
night. He was photographing an anniversary party until
two in the morning. I called his clients, and they backed
up his story. And Sunday night, he was at his computer,
working on a series of prints to hand in the next day. The
edit times on his machine, as well as two e-mails he sent
correspond with what he told us. It doesn't appear that he
had anything to do with the recent attacks."

"That doesn't clear him of Jean-Baptiste Cassian's
murder," Magistrate Becker said.

"Tim's a pretty typical loser. That's true," Kriven said. "But I can't really see him as a murderer."

"In a moment of anger, perhaps?" Becker asked.

"I have trouble imagining him killing his sister's fiancé and then burying him in the park," Kriven said. "He doesn't have the sangfroid for it. I don't even know if he has the smarts for it."

"Well, we do know that he's homophobic," Becker said. "Maybe he couldn't tolerate the fact that his sister was about to marry someone who was gay. That's a plausible motive."

"He used the word 'faggot,' but deep down, I don't think it's much of an issue for him," Rost said. "I don't even think he cared enough about his sister to keep her from marrying a man who, in the end, wouldn't make her happy. He cared about what he stood to gain. And Jean-Baptiste was the goose that laid the golden egg."

Becker let out a deep breath.

"What do you think?" he asked Nico.

"I'm inclined to agree with them. Tim Krall didn't do it."

"Franck? Are you done with all the banquet and excavation VIPs?" Nico asked.

"Yes, Chief," Captain Plassard said. "We saw the final witnesses last night. There's nothing to add."

"Okay, let's get to our scoop from the club," Nico said. "I'm sure Ayoub can't wait to tell you."

"Yes, let's," the magistrate said. "The investigation has exonerated Timothy Krall *a priori*."

"Gianni actually had some intriguing details to share—"

"And he only had eyes for the chief!" Ayoub interjected.

"Gianni definitely saw Clément Roux's attacker," Nico said, moving the conversation along. "He didn't especially like the man and thought he was manipulating the kid. But that's not the most interesting part. To describe him, Gianni used a term that struck me, because I heard Jean-Marie use the same term."

Everybody around the table was quiet. Nico had their attention. "Jean Marie, you described Mercier as a kind of pretty boy who wanted to come off as much younger than his fifty-two years."

"Yes, that was my impression," Rost said.

"And you called him a—"

"A little girl," Ayoub interrupted, looking at his boss.

"That's exactly the term Gianni used. We must find out if Mercier and the man Gianni saw at the club are one in the same."

Nico banged the table to emphasize his words. He was usually calm during these meetings, but not now.

"There was something else that struck me about the guy," Jean-Marie Rost said. He seemed to be thinking out loud.

"His voice," Becker suggested. "It was reedy, a bit higher-pitched."

"But someone's voice can be controlled and modified," Claire Le Marec pointed out. "That's why people take voice lessons. Furthermore, exhaustion and illness, the tone of a conversation, even switching from one language to another can change the pitch, volume, timbre, and tempo of someone's speech."

"It's still an integral part of our identity," Becker said. "Researchers have made progress there, with ways to do electronic voice recognition. Courts accept it as a form of identification. But we need some kind of comparison. If we had a recording of the attacker, the lab could compare his vocal imprint with Mercier's."

"But we have something else," Nico said mysteriously.

Everyone turned his way.

"A tic. Clément Roux's attacker kept rubbing his lower lip with the middle part of his finger. According to Dominique Kreiss, this kind of gesture is a very telling form of nonverbal communication. She's gone over this with us before: the face has seven key points, including the mouth, and caressing the lower lip is suggestive of a sexual impulse."

"I didn't notice that sort of gesture when I interviewed Mercier," Becker mused.

"Me either," Jean-Marie Rost said.

"There's only one conclusion I can draw from that," Kriven said. "You aren't Laurent Mercier's type."

"And right you are, David," Nico said, laughing.

"Evidently, Laurent Mercier is attracted to men who look like Jean-Baptiste Cassian," Becker said. "Let's say that you're right, Nico. What do you suggest?"

"The witnesses from the club and Clément Roux could identify the attacker's voice. It's worth a try, isn't it? With a clean setup, that index-finger tic could reappear and be an additional marker."

"And we'd be in a good position to get a confession," the magistrate acknowledged.

"Charlotte, any news on Mercier's alibi the night of Mathieu Leroy's attack?" Nico asked.

"The bar at the Hôtel du Louvre had so many customers, the employees couldn't be sure if they'd seen the man and his clients Tuesday night. If Mercier paid the bill with his credit card, we'd have a trail. But we'll have to wait until the banks open. As for his clients, I tried to get in touch but couldn't reach them. On Wednesday and Sunday night, we only have his wife's testimony, and I'm not convinced that she's trustworthy."

"Is it time to search their place?" Becker asked.

Val-de-Marne, where Vincennes was located, was a Paris suburb that was under the jurisdiction of the Paris police. That would make things easier.

"We'll need a search warrant and warrant for Laurent Mercier's arrest," Nico confirmed. "I'd also like to see Daniel Vion again and keep Tim Krall here. Three suspects for a lineup. What do you think?"

"That's fine. I'll draw up the warrants."

"Get ready," Nico told his team. "It's going to be a busy day."

The Rue Jean-Moulin in Vincennes was a narrow one-way street not far from the Château de Vincennes. The Merciers lived at number 17, a rambling house with blindingly white walls. A plaque read "Laurent Mercier, Certified Landscape Designer."

The unmarked police cars parked in the street, blocking the morning traffic. The officers didn't use their sirens or flashing lights. Nico wanted to approach the house as quietly as possible. Kriven's and Maurin's groups got out of their cars quickly. They were wearing bulletproof vests and carrying their Sig Sauger SP 2022s, nine-millimeter semiautomatic pistols. Each one had fifteen bullets and weighed about two pounds. Not as heavy as the old Manurhin revolver, which was now retired.

Nico's men had sangfroid and reflexes, and they knew that there were three children in the house.

A gated entry for cars in the middle of the building opened to an interior courtyard. From there, they would make their way to the office and the secondary entrance to the house, which had a garden. The goal was to control all the exterior spaces to prevent anyone's escape to the Rue d'Estienne-d'Orves or the Avenue de Paris. Commander David Kriven and his troops rushed into the courtyard as discreetly as possible. On the street, a small set of steps hidden behind a low wall led directly to the family home. Nico went up the steps while Commander Charlotte Maurin and Captain Ayoub Moumen kept a safe distance. The three other members of their group stood along the front wall, ready to break a window and demonstrate their authority if needed. Finally, Nico rang the Merciers' doorbell. It was breakfast time.

The chief heard chairs scraping the floor, muffled voices, and footsteps in the vestibule.

"Yes?" a woman asked behind the door. It was probably Camille Mercier.

"Good morning, ma'am. I'm Chief Sirsky of the Criminal Investigation Division. Can you open the door, please?"

Silence. Then a barely audible whisper. She was trying to get her husband.

"Mrs. Mercier?" Nico asked again. "I have a warrant to search the premises as part of a criminal investigation. You are under obligation to grant entry. I hope that we can do this peacefully. There are minors inside. But if you don't open the door, I will be required to use force."

A line from Blaise Pascal ran through his head. "Justice without power is inefficient, and power without justice is tyranny."

A key turned in the lock, and the door opened. Camille Mercier, wearing pajamas, seemed frightened. Nico handed her the search warrant. Commander Maurin mounted the steps and closed ranks behind her boss. The lady of the house stepped aside in resignation, and Laurent Mercier approached with a relaxed smile.

"Chief, to what do we owe the pleasure of your visit?" he asked in a toneless voice.

A finely chiseled face, Deputy Chief Rost had said. A nice ass and a nicer face. Yes, Nico could see what Rost had meant.

"The investigation into Jean-Baptiste Cassian's murder."

"That old thing? Again? I've managed to move past that sad affair, which hurt Camille and me so much."

"Sorry to bother you, Mr. Mercier. But we believe this murder is connected to more recent attacks."

"What does it have to do with my family?"

"You were among the victim's closest friends. I have a search warrant signed by the magistrate."

"A search warrant? Forgive my ignorance, but I don't know what you're getting at."

The man was extraordinarily calm, just as he'd been when Rost and Becker had stared him down.

"We also have a warrant for your arrest."

"An arrest warrant for me?" Mercier asked, clearly taken aback.

"Now!" Nico yelled to his teams. They had talked enough. It was time to act.

"Where are your children, Mrs. Mercier?" he asked.

"I sent them to their rooms to get ready for school."

"Can somebody in your family take them to school this morning?"

"Why would that be necessary?" Laurent Mercier asked.

His wife didn't say anything. She was looking at the floor.

"If not, our agents will go with them and then take your spouse to headquarters for questioning."

"I thought I was the one you wanted."

"Your wife is being brought along as a witness. I would suggest that you get ready, ma'am."

Commander Maurin followed Camille Mercier to make sure she didn't destroy or hide any evidence. The investigators would scour the house.

Nico asked Laurent Mercier to wait in the kitchen and assigned an officer to watch him.

Twenty minutes later, Mrs. Mercier and her three teenagers came downstairs. Two officers followed them.

Nico had gone into the kitchen and was inspecting the drawers and cabinets with a calculated slowness and false concentration as a clearly anxious Laurent Mercier looked on.

"Over here!" he heard Franck Plassard shout.

"Where?" Kriven responded from the living room.

"In the basement! Chief, we need you."

"What's in the basement?" Nico asked Mercier.

"A game room," the man replied. "With a bar, couches, a billiards table, a CD player, a television, and a console."

"Nothing else?"

"Chief?" Kriven had come upstairs again and had joined Nico in the kitchen.

"I'll come in a minute."

Kriven left, and Nico looked Mercier in the eye.

"What else?" he repeated.

"A lab."

"A photo lab, is that what you mean?"

"Yes," Mercier confessed.

Nico left him with the officer guarding him. He went down the stairway to the basement dark room. Kriven and Plassard were looking at the prints pinned on a clothesline. Although practically all photographers were now using digital methods, some professionals, as well as hobbyists, still preferred the older way, which involved processing film in a room with only a red light. They considered it more creative and satisfying. Mercier had a fully equipped darkroom with enlarger, developing tanks, tongs, paper, and chemicals.

"Portraits," Kriven observed.

"So that's his hobby," Plassard said. "But unlike Vion, he doesn't take group and travel photos."

"He's good. His angles are well-framed and thought-out."

"If Mercier is Jean-Baptiste Cassian's photographer, then maybe he kept a souvenir," Nico whispered. "Let's find it."

He knew they had to work fast. Anya would be going into the operating room at any minute now.

31

Nico sat on the couch facing Samuel Cassian. On the coffee table, his wife had set out refreshments, as always: tea, coffee, chocolate, slices of cake, and cookies. The ceremony didn't bother the artist, who played the game patiently and lovingly. Then he sent his wife away on a ruse. After so many years, he still wanted to spare her needless suffering. Nico respected him for that.

"I can still see myself on the Rue de Valois, in the gilded offices of André Malraux and the minister of culture," Samuel Cassian reminisced. "We were smoking Partagas. Jacques Langier took me out on the terrace overlooking the Palais Royal's gardens. He was proud of the palace courtyard; they had replaced the parking lot with the *Colonnes de Buren*, Daniel Buren's art installation. It was so long ago, but I remember it like it was yesterday. Bernard Tschumi was with us. He unfolded the map of the Parc de la Villette so we could decide where the banquet would take place."

"And you picked the Prairie du Cercle to the north of the Canal de l'Ourcq," Nico said. "There was no changing your mind."

A smile played on Samuel Cassian's face as he looked at the police chief.

"The City of Blood and Fear. Quite the foreshadowing, wasn't it? One second and your life is flipped upside down. Your son disappears, and you disappear along with him. My wife lost her mind, and sometimes I wish I had too."

His eyes had a strange glow.

"Your wife always believed that Jean-Baptiste left the country," Nico said. "She thought he'd rather flee than face the idea that he'd never be your equal. Or perhaps it was the other way around, and he was terrified of surpassing you."

"Yes, she preferred to believe that he went to the United States and was living a happy life in anonymity. She's told me this many times. She's even convinced that she has grandchildren. My God. I wish I could believe it myself."

The old man closed his eyes for a few seconds. Nico could see that he was struggling to avoid betraying his emotions. Once again, Nico laid out each of the group photos on the coffee table. He knew he was rubbing salt in the wound, but he didn't have a choice.

"Mr. Cassian..."

"Call me Samuel. Samuel would be nice. You remind me of my son. He was committed to his work too."

Nico looked away. This man had lost his son. Was he himself about to lose his mother? It was strange how their fates had aligned.

"Samuel, the man behind these prints was a friend of your son: Daniel Vion. Jérôme Dufour told him that your wife believed Jean-Baptiste was living abroad. Laurent Mercier, who's here in this picture, told him. So I have a question: How did Laurent Mercier know what your wife thought?"

"Oh, that's easy. Laurent came to visit us many times after Jean-Baptiste's disappearance. He was distraught."

"Was Laurent a family friend?"

"No, not really. But he was very close to our son."

"What makes you say that?"

"My wife would always fill him with sweets when he visited," Samuel Cassian replied with an affectionate smile. "Then he'd ask to go see Jean-Baptiste's room. He'd spend ten minutes or so in there all by himself. I didn't think this ritual was very healthy, but the young man seemed genuinely overwhelmed, and I hoped it would give him some comfort. I also hoped that his visits would taper off. They didn't, so I had to put an end to it."

Nico set his folder on the couch and drank some coffee. He wasn't hungry. He felt tired, not because of the long night at the club or because of all the time and energy he had put into solving this case. It was the thought of giving Samuel Cassian a final blow that was wearing him down.

"Samuel, I have something important to tell you."

His host sat up.

"I'm listening. I loved Jean-Baptiste, and nothing could change how much I loved him. Nothing, you hear me?"

Nico thought of Dimitri and knew he felt the same way. Was that what it meant to be a good father?

"Jean-Baptiste was cheating on Lara."

It was then that he saw that Samuel Cassian was holding a rosary. He was working the beads.

"At the time, Lara knew, but she wanted to go ahead and marry Jean-Baptiste," Nico continued.

"He was a young man. Those things happen."

"This case was, well, different."

"Don't beat around the bush, Chief."

"Call me Nico, please."

"I'm listening, Nico."

"He had been involved with another man."

The rosary fell to the floor. Samuel Cassian's face paled, but he managed to maintain his composure.

"Why didn't he tell me?" he asked. "I accepted everything about him. It wouldn't have mattered. Laurent—is that who you're thinking of? I caught him with his nose buried in one of Jean-Baptiste's sweaters. He was crying. My God, I should have known."

"The investigation isn't over, but I should have an answer for you very soon. Thank you for helping me, Samuel."

"No, Nico. Thank you. It sounds like you're close to arresting our son's murderer."

"We're closing in, yes. We hope to have something for you soon."

"Soon," the artist repeated, as if a theater curtain were about to fall.

So Samuel Cassian understood that the young man he had taken into his home and comforted, that this young man had done the unforgivable.

From his window, Samuel Cassian watched the chief's car pull away and merge with traffic between the Café de Flore and the Saint-Germain-des-Prés church. He wished it was his son in that car, the son he had missed every day for thirty years.

Why had Jean-Baptiste kept that vital part of himself a secret? What kind of mess had he gotten into that someone would kill him? If only he'd come to his father, things would have gone differently. But Samuel had no way of knowing that for sure.

Samuel rocked back and forth and pressed his head against the windowpane.

"Sweetheart, are you okay?" his wife asked nervously.

"I'm fine, darling."

"The police officer?"

"He left."

"I know. Just like I knew our son was dead the day he disappeared."

Samuel turned around.

"What did you think, Samuel? That I really believed Jean-Baptiste would leave us to go live in America? How could you think I was that far gone?"

Their eyes met, and his softened as he tried to read his wife's dark gaze.

"Even if Jean-Baptiste had fled to America, he would have found some way to let us know that he was all right.

He would have sent us a postcard, at least. But we've both known all this time that he never left the country."

Samuel pursed his lips. Those few seconds of clarity that flowed every so often through his wife's mind would fade away, and she would go back to her imaginary and orderly world. A world where their son lived forever on the other side of the Atlantic Ocean.

Samuel glanced at his watch. What time was it in New York? He closed his eyes. If only forgetfulness or madness could save him.

32

On the fourth floor of headquarters, the excitement was palpable. Tension, too, which was always felt just before the conclusion of an investigation. The division's finest had put together the pieces of the puzzle: Timothy Krall in custody, Laurent Mercier in the next cell over, Camille Mercier and Daniel Vion in interview rooms.

Nico walked into his office, along with Becker and the top officers.

"Mercier's alibi for the night Mathieu Leroy was attacked has fallen apart," Deputy Chief Rost said. "Camille's story is full of holes and inconsistencies."

"Mercier settled his tab at Le Defender with his credit card at twelve thirty in the morning," Commander Charlotte Maurin said. "According to the clients they spent the evening with, everyone left the Hôtel du Louvre and went their separate ways. The security guards at the Parc de la Villette discovered Mathieu Leroy around two in the morning, which gave Mercier plenty of time to commit the crime. The student was probably looking forward to a hot meeting. Instead, he met an animal. I'd say he was like the ones they used to sell at La Villette's markets, but those animals weren't predators."

"We've done voice recordings for Laurent Mercier, Daniel Vion, and Timothy Krall," Jean-Marie Rost said. "Gianni and Théo should be arriving at any minute now. Charlotte's group is getting ready for them."

"As soon as Clément Roux is well enough to listen, we'll pay him a visit at the hospital," Maurin added. "I understand he's recovering."

"Great. Here's the plan," Nico said, turning to Alexandre Becker.

Caroline's text caught his attention: "Anya won't be operated on until the end of the morning. Don't worry. She's in good hands. And Alexis and Tanya are here with me. They're letting us keep her company until she goes in. Then we'll stay till she wakes up. Don't forget: I love you."

"We're going to let Tim stew in his cell," Nico continued. "Plassard is dealing with Daniel Vion. We need to make sure he tells us everything; maybe he knows something else about Mercier. David, you're being assigned to the wife. Be cold and scare her. If her husband is the man we think he is, she'll break down. She needs to spill the beans."

Everybody nodded.

"Jean-Marie, you're in charge, and you'll collect all the information."

"What about Laurent Mercier?" Becker asked.

"I'd like to take him myself," Nico answered.

The magistrate was required to interrogate any suspect charged in a crime that he was investigating. He could authorize police officials to interrogate any suspect who hadn't been charged, as well as those who were close to a case, such as witnesses. Technically, the landscape designer hadn't been charged yet. Nico was counting on Becker to give him the go-ahead.

"Let me do it, and you'll have the signed confession this morning," he told Becker.

Becker nodded. "I'll be in my office. Keep me informed."

"No problem."

As everyone else streamed out of Nico's office, Becker stayed behind. "You aren't yourself this morning," he said, touching Nico's arm.

Nico hesitated. Could he tell his friend about the pact he'd made with fate?

"I'm sorry, Alex," he said. "I'm worried about my mother."

"She'll be okay. I'm sure of it," his friend assured him. "My wife spoke with Caroline last night, and she was confident."

"I'll feel better once she's out of the hospital."

"I understand."

"We'll hit the jackpot if our witnesses and Clément Roux positively ID Mercier's voice," Nico said.

"But we both know that's not enough. We need more than a vocal match to make a case that a good lawyer won't punch holes through."

"We also have the photos that we found at the suspect's house. They're just like the photos of Jean-Baptiste."

"You think Laurent Mercier was Jean-Baptiste Cassian's lover?"

"Why not? His wife and Daniel Vion may have the answer to that question. And I've got one last trick up my sleeve."

"Oh?" Alexandre Becker stared at him. He knew Nico had a flair for suspense.

"I'm keeping that a secret." The chief winked at him.

Charlotte Maurin received Gianni and Théo in the small office she shared with Captain Moumen. Gianni had traded his see-through mesh shirt for an impeccable Jean Paul Gaultier suit and tie.

"We have a real lead here," she told them.

"One of the guys from the pictures?" Théo asked. "I didn't recognize any of them."

"We're not focusing on the way Clément Roux's friend looked, but rather on how he sounded."

"How he sounded?" Théo asked.

"I'm going to play three recordings for you and ask you to listen. Tell me if you recognize one of the voices. Listen carefully. You must be absolutely sure."

"We're ready," Gianni replied calmly.

Moumen grabbed his computer mouse, opened the audio window, and started playing the recordings. The first voice rang out in the office. The two witnesses leaned forward in their chairs.

The two officers exchanged glances in the hallway. Then Captain Plassard went into the room where Daniel Vion was waiting. Commander Kriven shut the door behind him in the room where Camille Mercier was being held. They were determined to glean what they could from Laurent Mercier's friend and spouse.

Kriven immediately saw how fragile the woman was. She was huddled in her chair, and Kriven sensed that she wanted to disappear, to forget the father of her children and the miserable life he'd put her through. That was what Nico had implied. It was up to him to find out if this assessment was correct.

"Mrs. Mercier, your husband is suspected in the murder of Jean-Baptiste Cassian."

She bit her lip and was blinking quickly, a telltale sign of anxiety.

"Were you and Laurent lovers before your friend's disappearance?"

She sat up straight. Her hands were trembling.

"Not yet." Her voice was hoarse. "But I loved him."

"And did he love you?" Kriven asked.

"Would he have married me if he didn't?"

Who was she trying to convince?

"How long have you two been married, Mrs. Mercier?"

"Twenty-seven years."

"And how would you describe your relationship as a couple?"

She didn't seem to understand the question.

"Has your sexual relationship with your husband seemed normal to you?" Kriven pressed.

Her face turned red and then went ashen.

"Of course!" she shot back.

Too insistent to be honest.

"Laurent has always been preoccupied with his work," she said. "And it's demanding, so he tends to get tired. But I understand. He works hard to give us a good life."

She didn't look like she believed what she was saying.

"How is he with the children?"

"He's a good father. He's always there for them."

Clearly, Laurent Mercier didn't have much time for his wife.

"You and your husband have the same degree, but your name isn't on the plaque at the entrance. Why?"

"Oh, he's the one who runs everything. I'm just happy to help out when he's got too much on his plate."

Her statement contradicted what their clients had said. They said Mercier exploited his wife.

"That's not what we found when we talked with your clients. Laurent actually relies on you quite a bit, doesn't he?"

Camille was visibly embarrassed by the question.

"Is Laurent often absent in the evenings?" Kriven asked, changing the subject.

"Not at all. He enjoys spending time with his family. But sometimes he has to see clients in the evening."

"And what about the other evenings?"

"He often works late in his office."

"And that doesn't seem odd to you? Have you ever suspected that he looks at websites? At porn or hookup sites?"

She opened her mouth slightly.

"Jean-Baptiste was gay. Did you know that?" Kriven asked.

She rocked back and forth in her chair. She looked panicked.

"He had a lover, and we think the lover is the photographer who took these pictures of him," Kriven said as he set the prints on the table. "Do they look familiar?"

She shook her head emphatically.

"They demonstrate the same techniques your husband's skilled at, wouldn't you say?"

Camille was paralyzed.

What had Dominique Kreiss said? That if he was right, Camille Mercier was a submissive wife controlled by a tyrannical husband. Over the years, he had beaten her down to the point where she felt that she amounted to nothing on her own. She had become entirely dependent on him and didn't think she could live without him. And so whatever he did, she would justify his actions.

Why had Laurent Mercier opted to live a cruel lie? Same-sex marriage had been legal in France for a while, but society was much less tolerant at the time Laurent Mercier and his friends were going to school. Being gay wasn't accepted in the straight world, and many men felt compelled to marry women in an effort to reject their sexual orientation or cover it up. And men who had a real desire to father children were practically forced to marry women. Some gay men, pressed into pursuing lives that were dishonest at best, became mean-spirited and made their wives suffer for their bad choice.

"Haven't you ever thought about going through his computer and personal things to see what he's been hiding from you?" Kriven said. "An affair, maybe?"

"Yes," she said in a tight voice.

Nico took Laurent Mercier out of his cell and walked him to the interview room with a guard at their side. His

Sig Sauer was clearly visible on his belt. That always made an impression.

"Mr. Mercier, as you know, we found your darkroom. We also found your photographs," Nico said as soon as they sat down. "Our specialists have looked at them and will tell us if, based on their resemblance, you're the person who took the photographs of Jean-Baptiste Cassian."

"Those portraits are at least thirty years old," the suspect said, his tone still emotionless.

"The style and technical aspects of the photographs all bear a resemblance. You might even be using the same camera."

"Even if I took those photographs, what does that prove?"

"Why hide it from us?"

"I was afraid you'd get the wrong idea and waste your time. If I'd confessed that I was the photographer, you'd have put me at the top of your list. But I'm innocent. I had nothing to do with Jean-Baptiste's disappearance."

"So are you saying that you took these pictures?"

"Yes," he said with exasperation.

The two men sized each other up.

"I know you're proud of your work, Mr. Mercier," Nico said carefully. "And you've helped us with our investigation. Did you, by any chance, save the negatives?"

Nico noticed how Mercier's pupils were dilated, and his jaw was clenched.

"Those photographs are very old. I get rid of the negatives when they're a year or two old. If I kept all of my negatives, I would quickly run out of space."

"What kind of relationship did you have with Jean-Baptiste Cassian when you took those photos?"

"He was a friend."

"Yes, but his disappearance hit you especially hard, considering that you frequently visited his parents."

"I wanted to comfort them."

"I got the impression that you were the one who sought out Samuel Cassian and his wife and that they were kind enough to take you in."

"I'd just lost a friend."

"*Lost?*"

"A disappearance is a loss, is it not?"

"You would go into his room by yourself. That's an odd thing to do, wouldn't you say?"

"That was my way of dealing with it. I didn't want to let him go. I felt like I could be close to him in his room."

"You needed to smell his skin, his scent?"

Laurent Mercier didn't flinch. Just then, the guard opened the door. Deputy Chief Rost came in without paying any attention to the suspect. He gave his boss a paper folded in half. He left just as quickly. "Gianni and Théo have positively identified Laurent Mercier's voice. There was no question. Charlotte is on her way to the hospital. The doctors say Clément can listen to the recordings."

Nico read the message slowly to keep his suspect off balance.

"We have witnesses," he said calmly.

It was time to get serious.

"What did you find, Mrs. Mercier?" Commander Kriven asked.

"Folders on his computer," she whispered in a hurried, nervous tone.

"What was in those folders?"

"Photos. Porn. Men together." Kriven's colleagues were analyzing Mercier's hard drive and already had proof of what his wife was saying.

"Did you find anything else?" Kriven asked.

"E-mails. Laurent was meeting men." Anger and disgust were evident on Camille Mercier's face. She was a wounded woman.

Kriven swallowed. He had gotten what he wanted.

"Laurent Mercier is starting to go weak," Nico told Jean-Marie Rost. "How's everything going at your end?"

"Plassard's done with Daniel Vion. He confessed that he suspected something was up with Jean-Baptiste and Laurent. But he wasn't sure, and he was close to both Lara and Camille. He didn't want to say anything. He's still in custody."

"Mercier should be nervous about his old friend being in the room next to his. Is David still with Mrs. Mercier?"

"He's been with her the whole time. It's getting good. She went through her husband's computer and found gay porn. She's spilling all his dirty secrets right now."

"Perfect. It's time for the lineup."

The Paris police headquarters had changed little since the 1931 publication of Georges Simenon's first crime novel about Jules Maigret. The police didn't have modern rooms conforming to twenty-first-century standards. The holding cells on the third floor were used. So the hallway lights had to be dimmed to keep suspects from seeing witnesses. And the witnesses had to talk quietly, because there wasn't any soundproofing. The whole set-up was a far cry from the public perception of a police headquarters.

"We're going to do this another way," Nico said. "Set up a table in the room so that five men can sit side by side facing the one-way mirror."

"Five," Rost said. "That means Mercier, Vion, Krall, and two of our colleagues."

"Perfect. I've also asked Michel Cohen to find us a young guard about the same height and weight as Jean-Baptiste Cassian and the victims from the Parc de la Villette. He'll face the suspects, and we'll put him in charge of the interrogation. Michel Cohen should be preparing him and the two officers right now."

"How sneaky!" said Rost said.

Twenty minutes later, Michel Cohen, Jean-Marie Rost, David Kriven, Pierre Vidal, and Ayoub Moumen were all squeezed around Nico behind the one-way mirror. Gianni and Théo, the witnesses from the nightclub were let in, and Gianni gave the chief a hearty handshake. A few moments later, the young brown-haired guard who was to play the role of interrogator arrived.

"Go on in," Nico whispered to him.

He was a guy who knew how to handle himself, Cohen had said. And he looked cool in his jeans and tennis shoes. They trusted him to do the job.

He stepped into the lion's den. Mercier, Vion, Krall, and the two recruited officers were in place, with numbered placards in front of them.

"Gentlemen, let me explain why you're here," the interrogator began, looking them over one by one as he pulled out his chair.

Cohen had told him to play seducer.

"We're here for an identification. Behind the mirror, witnesses are watching you. Keep in mind that you're being filmed," he said, sitting down and crossing his legs.

He paused to let the words sink in.

"Do not say a single word," he said firmly.

He didn't want Laurent Mercier's voice to influence the witnesses.

"You can answer my questions by nodding or shaking your head. Do you understand?"

The five men nodded.

"Number One, are you familiar with the Parc de la Villette?" This man was one of their police officers. He nodded. "Do you visit the park?" Another nod.

"Number Two, are you married?" Daniel Vion shook his head. "Do you have children?" He did not.

"Number Three, do you live in Paris?" Timothy Krall nodded. He seemed shaky.

"Number One, do you live in Paris?"

Laurent Mercier was waiting to be called, and the abrupt return to the first man seemed to make him nervous.

"Number Four, have you ever visited the Parc de la Villette?" The second police officer shook his head.

"Number Five, did you book a hotel room for one night near the Parc de la Villette?" The question was meant to up the ante. Mercier paused, then shook his head.

"Number One, did you spend a night in a hotel near the Parc de la Villette?" The cop nodded. The best was yet to come. "And was the room to your liking?"

"Wait," Gianni said.

"What do you see?" Nico asked. He leaned in to hear what the lawyer had to say.

"That gesture." He pointed to one of the suspects. "The guy who picked up Clément was doing exactly the same thing."

"I saw him do it, too," Théo said. He was thoroughly absorbed in the drama unfolding on the other side of the one-way mirror.

"Number Five, are you married?" Mercier nodded. "Do you love your wife?"

Nico saw his unease. Gianni held up his fist.

"It's Number Five," he said quietly.

Mercier stroked his lip slowly with the middle of his finger.

"Now for the coup de grace," Nico said.

33

Michel Cohen walked down the long hallway and crossed the third-floor landing, which boasted a bay window and security monitors. Only a few people could access this level of headquarters. Farther off, he opened a door and walked into a comfortable waiting room with white walls and a hardwood floor. A bronze lamp with five lights held aloft by sculpted Nubians lit the room. It was a Louis XV: tacky and blatantly racist, Cohen knew. But the bureaucrats kept saying it was an antique and wouldn't change it. The waiting room opened onto his office and that of the chief of staff, who managed the records, paperwork, and statistics. From there, he entered the antechamber of his boss, Nicole Monthalet. He walked past the light well and the secondary stairwell leading to the different departments. Finally he entered office 210. The commissioner's secretaries gave him a wave. One of them held out an ashtray. Cohen crushed out his cigar before stepping into Mrs. Monthalet's office, the only place where he couldn't smoke.

"Have a seat, Michel," she said authoritatively. "How far along are we?"

"It's almost done."

"What did he have up his sleeve?"

"He's getting ready for it."

"Ah, he's a smart one, isn't he?" She smiled, and her eyes sparkled.

"He's a first-rate cop. That's for sure."

"I had to fight to keep him, did you know that? The minister of the interior wanted to snap him up."

"Sirsky wouldn't have wanted the job."

"How much longer can he stay at headquarters, though? I'm worried, Michel. We need him here."

"To accomplish the impossible," Cohen joked, knowing all too well that his boss used the term only when she was talking about Nico Sirsky. "You'll have proof of it on your desk later this morning. I'm sure of it."

Nicole Monthalet, the thorough professional who turned heads with her blonde good looks, nodded in agreement. Her expression became pensive. There had been a lot at stake in this case, which involved a famous artist, a world-renowned park, and a former minister of culture. The art world was watching, and government officials wanted the case closed quickly and efficiently.

"Mr. Mercier, we've looked at your digital files," Becker said. "We've found pornographic photos and particularly suggestive e-mails."

Laurent Mercier kept his head up, but he had taken a serious blow.

"We know you've had extramarital affairs."

"I wasn't aware this was a crime."

"We've learned that Jean-Baptiste Cassian had a relationship with a man," Becker continued. "And from everything we've gathered, we have reason to believe it was with you."

"Do you have any proof?"

"Your wife told us," Nico said. "She was very clear on that point. She also suspects you of murdering your friend."

"You're crazy."

"Jean-Baptiste had decided to break things off with you and marry Lara," Becker continued. "You were hurt and angry. But in your eyes, it wasn't just his relationship with Lara that stood in the way. It was Jean-Baptiste's fear of disappointing his father. So you murdered him and threw his body in with his father's work. It wasn't all that hard, after all. The tables, chairs, and implements had just been buried. All you had to do was wait until dark. The soil was still loose and easy to dig up. Once the job was done, you just smoothed over the dirt and walked away."

"But even then, after you murdered and buried your former lover, your anger wasn't assuaged," Nico accused. "You married, had children, and managed to keep your anger under control, but it kept eating at you. And when you learned that Samuel Cassian's *tableau-piège* was being exhumed, your feelings welled up. Jean-Baptiste had rejected you in the worst way. It was something you had never gotten over, and you needed to lash out again. And so you seduced and assaulted three young men. They were just substitutes for Jean-Baptiste Cassian."

"Your alibis for the evenings when the attacks happened don't check out," Becker added. "But we have something better, Mr. Mercier. Proof, in fact."

"Witnesses recognized your voice," Nico said. "Especially your last victim, who survived."

Laurent Mercier blanched. He hadn't expected Clément Roux to live.

"In addition, you have a habit of rubbing your finger over your lower lip. Our witnesses saw you doing it. This tic has betrayed you."

"What do you have to say for yourself?" Becker asked.

"I'd say you don't have anything on me," Mercier said quickly.

"We'll see," Nico said, giving him a knowing smile. He got up to leave the room. "We've saved a little surprise for you."

In the Coquibus room, they were watching the scene on a webcam. Claire Le Marec, Jean-Marie Rost, Kriven and Maurin's groups, and the psychologist Dominique Kreiss were all glued to the screen and hanging on every word of the interrogation.

"Shit, he's good!" Vidal said.

"He's going to nail that bastard," Moumen added.

"Look!" Plassard said. He'd just come out of his office.

"This is when it happens," Deputy Chief Rost said.

"It's going to be a bloodbath," Kriven said.

"Here they come…" Maurin whispered as they all watched.

There was no time to lose. Nico came in first, with the woman on his heels. When Laurent Mercier saw her, the blood drained from his face.

"Lara." His voice trembled.

"You remember Lara Krall, Jean-Baptiste's fiancée?" Becker asked without waiting for a response. "Ma'am, do you recognize Laurent Mercier?"

"Yes, I recognize him."

Despite everything she'd gone through, she was calm, as Nico had advised her to be.

"Just before his disappearance, Jean-Baptiste confessed that he had cheated on you. Is that correct?" Becker asked.

"I guessed it."

"What clued you in?"

"A bite on his shoulder that he tried to hide."

"What explanation did he give you?"

"That it was from a one-time fling."

Nico could see that Mercer was getting angry.

"'An artist sometimes feels the need to stretch himself creatively,' he told me." Her voice was full of scorn. "That meant being open to new experiences. He begged me to forgive him. He swore that he loved me and wanted to marry me."

"And have children with you," Nico said. "Is that right?"

Nico could see that Mercier was getting even angrier. Lara could give Jean-Baptiste children, and Mercier could never make Jean-Baptiste happy in that way.

"He didn't want children," Mercier said.

"Of course he did," Lara Krall shot back.

The dialogue played out exactly as Nico had hoped.

"Never, you slut!" Mercier shouted. He rose from his chair, his two hands planted on the table. "Jean-Baptiste would never have knocked you up, not you, not anyone else! He was mine!"

The silence was oppressive. Tears rolled down Lara Krall's cheeks while hate blazed in Mercier's eyes.

"You were just a fleeting whim," Nico said to Mercier. "He didn't need you."

"What do you know, you schmuck?" The pitch of his voice was rising. "We loved each other. I wanted us to go to New York. We could have lived there happily. But Jean-Baptiste was too afraid to come out. He thought it would ruin his reputation."

"You fought."

"He dared... He dared to call me crazy. Apparently I made him want to hurl. After all those nights of lovemaking."

"So you took a hammer and hit him."

"I didn't want to. I..."

"You let him rot in that pit."

"He was so self-absorbed. And being a credit to his father was such an obsession. I didn't count for anything."

"Why did you assault the other young men?"

"All they wanted to do was shoot their load and leave, just like Jean-Baptiste. I made sure they wouldn't be able to ditch anyone else."

"Why did you bite their shoulders?"

"For Jean-Baptiste. He loved it when I did that."

Laurent Mercier had shot his own load. He had made his confession, and now he was slumped in his chair, an anguished look on his face.

"Take him away," Nico said.

His men came in and steered him out of the room.

"Thank you, Lara," Nico said. "You can go home with your brother."

"He's free?" she said.

"Yes," Alexandre Becker said. "Timothy may not have been entirely honest, but he didn't kill anyone."

The woman got up unsteadily.

"You should talk to someone about all this," Nico said. "It's a heavy burden, and you've carried it far too long."

Lara Krall didn't say anything. She shut the door behind her.

34

Applause and cheers rang out. The enthusiasm was evident. Everyone saluted their boss and his legendary intuition.

"A crime of passion. It's so banal in the end," Captain Plassard said.

"Ah, but is it?" Nico replied. "Samuel Cassian set out to redefine the limits of art and archaeology. But look what he dug up. Not only his son's remains, but also secrets that had been hidden for far too long. Now that they've been exposed, maybe all those who suffered because of Jean-Baptiste's disappearance can make peace with what happened and create better lives for themselves. That's not so banal, Franck."

In the midst of all the exuberance, a smiling face appeared in the doorway. It was Caroline. She made her way to him.

"Anya's operation went beautifully, and she's in recovery," Caroline whispered in his ear. "We were there when she woke up, and she wants to see you as soon as you can get to the hospital. I wanted to tell you in person, and I promised that I would drag you there, although I know I won't have to."

"Thank you. My God, thank you."

He took her in his arms and waved to his men. They understood that his mother was okay.

"She'll leave the hospital in eight days. And it looks like you've just closed your case. I'm so happy for you. You've been burying yourself in your work. Now maybe you can come up for air."

Nico would be able to collect material evidence over the next few days: how Mercier was able to attract his prey, the knife he used to stab them, the hammer he had probably saved like a relic… Maybe even the old souvenirs of his life with Jean-Baptiste.

"Boss?" Commander Charlotte Maurin called out. "I'd like to introduce you to someone."

She led him into the hallway. Nico didn't let go of Caroline's hand.

A young woman was waiting under the lit sign—like the ones at a train station—that announced the Criminal Investigation Division.

"Chief, please meet Élodie."

With a radiant smile, she shook the chief's hand and then Caroline's.

"Élodie is my fiancée," Commander Maurin said.

"It's a pleasure, Élodie. Welcome to La Crim'," Nico said. "Have Charlotte show you around. But before she does that, I just have just one thing to ask: please take good care of our commander here."

"I will," Elodie said.

Nico said good-bye to the pair and took Caroline down the narrow corridor to his office, where he could finally take her in his arms. And just as he was moving closer to breathe in her scent, a Jay-Z cover of "I'd Do Anything" popped into his head. Dimitri had been listening to it a few days earlier. Rap wasn't exactly Nico's genre, but the sentiment was spot-on.

"May I have this dance, ma'am?" he said as he opened his arms to her. She stepped into them and put her cheek next to his. Nico began humming. Yes, he'd do anything—everything—for her.

EPILOGUE

TWO WEEKS LATER

A revolution in point of view: something that looked entirely banal when viewed horizontally could become something fresh and innovative when viewed vertically. Surely that was one of Samuel Cassian's objectives—to capture a specific moment in time and invite people to stop what they were doing and see it from an entirely different perspective. Cassian had accomplished this and was ready to move on.

He had no way of knowing that his banquet burial would end not just a chapter in his life, but his whole life as he had known it.

"How could I have imagined that some crazy person would make my own child a prisoner of my art? That he'd murder my son and bury him in this trench?" Cassian ruminated as he stood with Nico in front of the pit, which was being filled for a final time.

Nico put his hand on the distraught old man's shoulder. The bones would be returned to Jean-Baptiste's family. Samuel and his wife would finally be able to give their son a proper burial in a site with a marker.

"We have a house in Sicily. A beautiful island," Cassian said. "Jean-Baptiste will be put to rest there."

The last cubic feet of dirt covered all traces of the banquet burial. Nico felt the man shaking.

"Justice has been served," Samuel said. He had been moved to tears. "Thank you."

"I was only doing my job, sir."

"Don't be so modest. Maigret can sleep soundly. He has a worthy successor."

Nico smiled.

"You're a good man, Nico. My son would have become one too, but he made an error in judgment that turned out to be fatal. I could have helped him."

"He didn't want to disappoint you."

"I wish he had thought more of me. Gay or straight, I loved him. And maybe if he had come out, I could have told him that his friend, Mercier, was the wrong person to be involved with."

"I know."

Nico thought of his own father, an amiable man, like the one he was talking with here.

"The Criminal Investigation Division has made an arrest in the thirty-year-old slaying of the son of well-known artist Samuel Cassian," a reporter told Parisians watching the afternoon news. "Charged with murder is Laurent Mercier, a school friend of Jean-Baptiste Cassian. The arrest was made just before the artist's dig at the Parc de la Villette was filled in again, after its exhumation."

Those at the site clapped as the banquet was buried for the final time. The journalists started jostling each other and shouting questions. Louis Roche, the head of park security, gave Nico a nod. But Nico's mind was elsewhere. He was already thinking about a new investigation. There was no respite in Nico's job: solving Paris homicides. Because it wasn't just a job. It was personal.

Thank you for reading The City of Blood.

We invite you to share your thoughts and reactions on Goodreads and your favorite social media and retail platforms.

We appreciate your support.

ACKNOWLEDGMENTS

The *tableau-piège* has been buried, and another page has been turned. I'd like to thank all those who have fed my imagination. Chief Nico Sirsky will always hold a special place for them in his heart.

Jean-Marie Beney, prosecutor at the Cour d'Appel of Dijon, and professor at the Université de Versailles Saint-Quentin-en-Yvelines.

Florence Berthout, general director of the Établissement Public du Parc et de la Grande Halle de la Villette.

Dr. David Corège, chief of emergency medicine in Saône-et-Loire and medical expert for the Cour d'Appel of Dijon.

Jean-Paul Demoule, former president of the Institut National de Recherches Archéologiques Préventives, member of the Institut Universitaire de France, professor of European protohistory at the Université de Paris I Sorbonne-Panthéon—UFR Art et Archéologie.

Valérie Ebersohl, archivist at the Établissement Public du Parc et de la Grande Halle de la Villette.

Tatiana Grigorieva, of the Centre Culturel de Russie de Paris.

Lucien Jougla, chief of security for the Établissement Public du Parc et de la Grande Halle de la Villette.

Henry Moreau, police commander, chief of staff for the director of the Police Judiciare of Paris.

Dr. Lionel Yon, orthopedic surgeon.

And Lilas Seewald, my dear editor at Fayard Noir.

A wink to Bernard Müller, doctor of social anthropology, in memory of the Société pour le Déterrement du *Tableau-Piège*, researcher at the Institut de recherche interdisciplinaire sur les enjeux sociaux.

And a special mention to the true artist, Daniel Spoerri, whose work and excavation of his *tableau-piège* inspired this novel.

ABOUT THE AUTHOR

Writing has always been a passion for Frédérique Molay. She graduated from France's prestigious Science Po and began her career in politics and the French administration. She worked as chief of staff for the deputy mayor of Saint-Germain-en-Laye and then was elected to the local government in Saône-et-Loire. Meanwhile, she spent her nights pursuing the passion she had nourished since penning her first novel at the age of eleven. After *The 7th Woman* took France by storm, Frédérique Molay dedicated her life to writing and raising her three children. She has five books to her name, with three in the Paris Homicide series.

About the Translator

Jeffrey Zuckerman was born in the Midwest and lives in New York. He has worked as an editorial assistant, a lifeguard, and a psychology researcher. Now an editor for *Music and Literature Magazine*, he also freelances for several companies, ranging from the pharmaceutical industry to old-fashioned book publishing. He holds a degree in English with honors from Yale University, where he studied English literature, creative writing, and translation. He has translated several Francophone authors, from Jean-Philippe Toussaint and Antoine Volodine to Régis Jauffret and Marie Darrieussecq, and his writing and translations have appeared in the *Yale Daily News Magazine, Best European Fiction,* and *The White Review.* In his free time, he does not listen to music.

About Le French Book

Le French Book is a New York-based publisher specializing in great reads from France. As founder Anne Trager says, "There is a very vibrant, creative culture in France. Our vocation is to bring France's best mysteries, thrillers, novels, and short stories to new readers across the English-speaking world."

www.lefrenchbook.com

Discover more books from

Le French Book

The Paris Lawyer by Sylvie Granotier
A psychological thriller set between the sophisticated corridors of the Paris courts and a small backwater in central France, where rolling hills and quiet country life hide dark secrets.
www.theparislawyer.com

The Winemaker Detective Series
by Jean-Pierre Alaux and Noël Balen
A total Epicurean immersion in French countryside and gourmet attitude with two expert winemakers turned amateur sleuths gumshoeing around wine country. Already translated: *Treachery in Bordeaux, Grand Cru Heist, Nightmare in Burgundy,* and *Deadly Tasting.*
www.thewinemakerdetective.com

The Greenland Breach by Bernard Besson
The Arctic ice caps are breaking up. Europe and the East Coast of the United States brace for a tidal wave. A team of freelance spies face a merciless war for control of discoveries that will change the future of humanity.
www.thegreenlandbreach.com

The Consortium Thriller Series by David Khara
A roller-coaster ride dip into World War II that races through a modern-day loop-to-loop of action. What impact could the folly of war—death camps, medical manipulation and chemical warfare—still have today?
www.theconsortiumthrillers.com

CPSIA information can be obtained at www.ICGtesting.com
Printed in the USA
BVOW08*1943050215

385811BV00003B/4/P